The Goblin's Bride

Silveri Sisters
Book 3

R. L. Medina

For all the middle children who've ever felt forgotten or unseen.
May you find your happily ever after.

People (and animals) of Zamerra

Signora Gloria Silveri (Mama)
The matriarch of the Silveri family. She is a seer who arrived in Zamerra with her five daughters and no husband. Meddlesome at times, she will do anything for her girls.

Alessia Silveri
The oldest of the Silveri daughters. Unlike her sisters, she has no magic, but she is the only one who can hear the enchanted villa speak. She is married to Massimo Gallo, a half-fae count, making her the Contessa of Zamerra and surrounding region.

Liliana Silveri
The second oldest of the Silveri daughters. Her magic skill is with brewing potions and performing spells. She is engaged to the warlock, Dante Lazzaro and runs the Apothecary in town.

Pamina Silveri
The third oldest and middle child of the Silveri family. She has baking magic and also makes the best, magical caffé.

Serafina Silveri (Fina)
The fourth daughter in the Silveri family. She can talk to and command animals.

Fiorella Silveri (Ella)
The youngest Silveri sister. She has plant and earth magic which she struggles to control at times.

Count Massimo Gallo
The half-fae count who would rather sit in his favorite chair with a book than make public speeches. He falls in love with the oldest Silveri sister, Alessia.

Dante Lazzaro
Massimo's best friend and skilled warlock. He helps his fiancé, Liliana, run the Apothecary.

Stefano Rivaldi
The tailor's son. He has set his sights on Pamina.

Signor Covelli
The town baker and deceased father of Lorenzo and Giulia.

Lorenzo Bartoli
The son and heir of Signor Covelli. He is a half-goblin who comes to Zamerra to claim his inheritance.

Giulia Bartoli

The daughter and heir of Signor Covelli. She accompanies her brother to town after her engagement falls through.

Salvatore Rossi

The Silveri's neighbor and friend. He is married to Adriano, a faun, and is the oldest of the Rossi brothers.

Adriano Rossi

Salvatore's faun husband. An introvert, he prefers to stay home and throw dinner parties. Heir to an enormous fortune, he and his husband are able to enjoy their quiet life just outside of Zamerra.

Angelo Rossi

The third oldest Rossi brother. An extrovert, he is often the spokesman for his family and has a fondness for Serafina Silveri.

Other characters:

Padre Leonardo

The ordained minister of Zamerra's only chapel.

Signora Bianchi

Signor Covelli's employee in the bakery.

Patrizio and Patrizia Foncello

The mayors of Zamerra. Together they oversee day to day things in the little town.

Signora Savelli

The matchmaker and busybody of Zamerra.

Ometta
   Dante's owl familiar.

Rafaelo Rossi
   The second oldest Rossi brother. He is quiet and reserved, taking after his father. He will inherit the Rossi goat and horse farm.

Marco Rossi
   The youngest of the Rossi family. He helps his brothers on their farm.

Bruno
   The Silveri's house elf.

Franny
   Alessia and Massimo's house elf.

Massimo's spoiled cat.

Gio
   The scrappy little dog that has become a part of the cat gang that lives in the Silveri's yard.

Fabrizio
   The Silveri's old horse.

Chapter 1

The Funeral

Pamina

C old bit through Pamina Silveri's wool coat as she stood with her family at the edge of the cemetery. Padre Leonardo's deep voice rose above them, carried by the autumn wind. Sniffles and coughs rippled through the crowd. It was that time of year when colds and other ailments ran rampant through Zamerra.

I'll need to make some stronger soup now. More garlic and ginger. A spell for decongestion.

Pamina's mind ran through all the recipes she knew and all the ingredients she'd need. Her fingers twitched inside her gloves, ready and eager to start.

The loss of Signor Covelli, the town's baker, had hit her hard and while she couldn't do anything about his passing, she could do what she did best—comfort and heal people through her food. Through her magic.

A shuffling sound came from beside her. Pamina opened one eye to see her younger sister, Serafina, growing restless as the Padre droned on.

Serafina caught her stare. "What?" she mouthed.

Pamina shook her head and put a finger to her lips in warning. Serafina was on the cusp of womanhood, nearly sixteen, but that didn't seem to stop her from acting out when bored. Even their youngest sister, Fiorella, at only ten, showed more decorum than Serafina sometimes.

"Amen," the adre finally finished.

"Amen," Pamina repeated along with everyone else.

Somewhere in the distance, a bird cawed as if echoing them. Pamina watched as the men lowered the coffin into the ground and covered it with dirt. Some of the townsfolk stepped forward to add their own handfuls.

A shudder ran through her. Poor man. With no family in town, his gravestone had been commissioned and paid for by Pamina's sister and brother-in-law, the count and contessa. The workers would set the stone another day and it would stand lonely, slightly apart from the family plots.

"Thanks to the hospitality of our count and contessa as well as the patrizia and I, there will be food served at the bakery for all. Please join us in remembrance of the late Signor Covelli," came Signor Foncello's, the town's patrizio, booming voice.

His wife, the patrizia, nodded serenely and motioned everyone toward town. People began to disperse, murmurs and whispers filling the silence.

Pamina's gaze swept across the somber faces, looking for one she didn't recognize. The whole town of Zamerra had come out. All but the ones who were too under the weather to leave their bed. The contessa, her sister, along with her husband were also absent, having been called away on important business.

A chill that had nothing to do with the cold settled in Pamina's chest. Why hadn't Signor Covelli's family come? Didn't he have anyone left?

The older man had always been kind to her and her family, which was more than she could say for some of the other townsfolk. Not everyone could overlook the Silveri girls' scandalous patronage. Though her older sisters, Alessia and Liliana, shared the same father, Pamina and her younger two sisters did not. That and the fact that their mother was a known seer and Liliana brewed potions and could perform spells made the Silveris the frequent target for gossip.

Pamina's own magic, with food, was not much of a secret either. However nobody outside her family knew the extent of her power. Pamina wasn't sure she even knew the depths of her baking and cooking magic.

"Mama, can we stay for the party?" Fiorella's voice brought Pamina back to the present.

Serafina snorted. "It's not a party, Ella. A man is dead."

Fiorella's face flushed.

"It's called a reception," Pamina said, casting Serafina a scolding look.

Their mother nodded and drew Fiorella to her side. "Yes, amore. We should pay our respect to Signor Covelli."

Serafina followed them, blowing out a loud breath. "I thought that's what we just did."

Pamina frowned at her rudeness. Usually, Serafina looked for any excuse to go into town, but lately, she'd been so sullen and ornery about everything. Maybe after some of Pamina's enchanted cannoli, her mood would improve.

"Signorina Silveri, I hope to see you at the reception." A voice caught Pamina's ear.

She turned to see a familiar, handsome face. Stefano Rivaldi, the tailor's son, gave her an appraising look. Heat spread across Pamina's face at his frank stare.

"Yes, I'll be there, Signor. Such a pity about poor Signor Covelli. And that his family couldn't make it," she said, straightening out her skirt as she walked.

"Hmm. Yes. Pity," Stefano replied as he elbowed his way

through the throng of people to catch up with her. Behind him, his friends smirked and whispered together in their direction.

Pamina's pulse quickened as Stefano joined her. He stood a foot taller than her and walked with a purposeful air. He was the handsomest of the eligible men in Zamerra and he knew it.

Though Pamina and her family lived just outside the town, she knew all the rumors about him. She'd heard about the many young women he'd left brokenhearted.

Just as she knew he'd probably heard all the talk about her and her family. Witches. Fatherless. Scandalous. Though her older sister marrying the count had improved their status a little.

Stefano grinned at her, his sea green eyes lighting on her chest. Pamina's face warmed. The black cotton blouse fit her rather snugly, but it was still modest. She'd inherited her mother's generous curves and thick waist and while some people were rude about it, it also seemed to draw a lot of unwanted male attention.

"Pamina!" a voice called ahead.

She looked up to see her sister, Liliana, waiting for her. Her sister's fiancé, Dante Lazzaro, stood beside her.

"I didn't see you two at the gravesite. Were you there?" Pamina asked as she caught up to them.

Dante smiled warmly at her and nodded. "Of course. How could we miss it? It's all everyone's been talking about as if it's the most exciting thing to happen in Zamerra."

Her sister didn't answer. Her eyes were fixed on Stefano, her lips curled in distaste. To his credit, the young man only faltered once under her glare before bidding them farewell and hurrying to rejoin his friends.

Pamina watched him go with a mixture of relief and disappointment. Dante offered her his arm as they continued walking, one eyebrow arched at her curiously. "Friend of yours?"

Liliana, on his other arm, peered around him to frown at her. "What did Stefano want?"

"Nothing. He was just being friendly."

Liliana snorted. "Oh, I bet. You—"

"Please. Not here, Liliana," Pamina cut her off, heat searing her skin.

Dante gave her a sympathetic look, which only furthered her embarrassment. Ignoring her sister's questioning look, Pamina stared straight ahead.

She knew, deep down, that Stefano was trouble, but a part of her couldn't help but entertain the idea of them together. What if he could change? What if he actually did care for her?

Pamina glanced up at the dreary sky and shook off the questions. They had just buried poor Signor Covelli and here she was brooding over her marriage prospects. Or lack of prospects.

She looked over at Dante and her sister. Their eyes were locked together in a silent exchange. Liliana turned away first, but Dante continued to watch her, a smile on his lips. The adoring look he gave her sister made Pamina's chest tighten. Would a man ever look at her the same way?

Or was she doomed to become their mother, alone against the world? Or worse, would she end up like the poor baker with no legacy or children to mourn her when she passed?

"Santo Cielo," Pamina muttered, shaking her head at herself.

As soon as she arrived at the bakery, she'd help herself to a large mug of her special caffé. That would help clear her mind and emotions and hopefully bring her out of this strange funk she'd been in lately.

They passed the town's little stone chapel, leaves crunching under their boots as they walked. Voices murmured around them as they followed everyone to the dirt path that would lead them into the heart of Zamerra. A gust of wind blew past them, making Pamina shiver.

More and more, the warmth of the bakery and her magical caffé sounded perfect. She couldn't see her mother or younger sisters in the wave of people, but she would catch up to them once they reached the reception.

Smoke billowed from the chimneys of the clustered shops and homes, the scent growing stronger as they got closer. Dirt turned to cobblestones and soon the echo of everyone's boots drowned out the chatter and coughs.

"How is everyone going to fit in the bakery?" Pamina asked aloud.

"We've opened our potion shop for the reception as well," Dante answered her.

"Yes, and the patrizios have spread out tables and chairs in the plaza too," Liliana added.

As they made it to the center of Zamerra, Pamina could see the tables her sister spoke of. They surrounded the giant fountain, set up end to end, and were laden with trays and trays of various dishes. Savory and garlicky aromas of different pastas and soups filled the air along with the sugary scents of the pastries and pies.

The dishes Pamina had made and brought herself were nowhere to be seen. Perhaps they were still inside the bakery where she'd arranged them.

"Did Massimo tell you anything more about Signor Covelli's heir?" Liliana asked, glancing at her fiancé.

Her question caught Pamina's attention. She looked to Dante as well, waiting for his answer.

He shrugged. "Only that he'd be arriving soon. After the funeral."

"So, he does have an heir? We should have waited to hold the funeral. I'm sure he wanted to be here for it," Pamina said.

Dante looked at her, dark eyes gleaming. "Oh, no," he lowered his voice, "Massimo said the man made it pointedly clear that he did not want us to wait to bury the body. Apparently, there was no love lost between them."

Liliana frowned. "Or maybe he's coming from too far and understood the importance of burying a body quickly. Wait too long and the rot becomes unbearable."

A shudder ran through Pamina. "Liliana. You shouldn't speak of such things," she said.

Her sister scowled, brown eyes narrowing. "What? I haven't said anything too crass. Have I?" She glanced at her fiancé.

Dante grinned at her and winked. "Crass or not, you do have a way with words, amore."

Liliana gave him a playful shove, a small smile playing on her lips. Pamina looked away, feeling like an intruder in their moment. Dante's words rang in her ears.

Signor Covelli had an heir. An heir who would be coming to claim the bakery. Though she tried not to think badly of this stranger, she couldn't help but wonder if what Dante said was true.

Had there been some sort of falling out between Signor Covelli and his heir? Even so, she couldn't see how someone could miss the funeral of a family member. Perhaps, the man's grief had been too much.

She made a mental note to bake something fresh for his arrival. A special treat that would help soothe his sorrow. Maybe a pie.

"We should hurry or all the honey cakes will be gone," Dante said, pulling Pamina from her thoughts.

Liliana shook her head at him. "You and your honey cakes. I asked Pamina to make a tray special just for you. It's in our shop."

Dante turned to Pamina with a smile. "You are my favorite sister now. Don't tell the others."

Pamina smiled back, though her mind was still preoccupied with what she'd just learned about the baker's heir. What would he do with the little bakery?

Voices grew louder as they made their way through the plaza. The tantalizing smell of fresh caffé and sugary treats filled Pamina's lungs as they grew closer to the bake shop.

Everyone was crowding to get inside and escape the cold. Even with the torches and chimineas lit by the tables outside, the air was sharp and unrelenting.

"Come on, let's go into our shop," Liliana said, leading the way next door.

Dante let go of Pamina's arm and followed his fiancée. Ahead, Pamina spotted her mother and sisters already making their way there as well.

The bells rang as they walked through the door. Fire burned from the cast iron chiminea in the corner, filling the room with warmth. The distinct medicinal smell of the potions mixed with the dried herbs and floral perfumes made Pamina's nose itch.

"I figured the bakery would be too crowded and the plaza too cold, so I brought some of the dishes here," Liliana said, waving them all to the back kitchen.

Mama walked along with them and clucked her tongue. "Liliana, I thought you were opening the shop up to the townsfolk as well."

Liliana scoffed. "Well, yes, if they want to come in, I'll let them, but I'm not leaving the door open in this cold."

Pamina glanced at Dante, trying to gauge his reaction. The Apothecary was actually his shop, but after giving up his magic to save her sister, he had taken on the role of Liliana's helper, doing all the non-magical things that needed doing. Though he never said otherwise, he must have missed being a powerful warlock.

His sacrifice was admirable and romantic. Would she ever find a man who would love her as much as he loved Liliana?

"I brought some of Pamina's dishes too," Liliana said, catching her attention.

She gestured to the spread of food on their small table. There was a basket of freshly baked bread beside little plates of oil and balsamic vinegar, the tray of honey cakes, and various dishes of pasta and roasted vegetables.

Pamina frowned at the giant pot of her minestrone soup in the center. "I made this for the others, Liliana. They're the ones with the colds."

Her sister shrugged. "They can have whatever is left."

Not wanting to argue, Pamina walked over to the coat rack. She took off her heavy coat and hung it up along with the others. Fire blazed from the stone hearth behind them, cozy and warm. Garlic hung from hooks on the wooden rafters, its scent now muddled with the food Liliana had brought.

Shaking off her irritation at her sister, Pamina grabbed plates from the cupboard. Busying herself always helped keep her anxious thoughts and emotions at bay.

Fiorella rubbed her hands in front of the fire and sighed. "I wish Alessia and Massimo could be here."

"They'll be back soon enough," Mama said, wrapping her arms around her youngest and kissing the top of her head.

Serafina huffed as she sat down. "I wish they'd taken me with them. I want to meet the king."

Liliana, who'd been helping Pamina plate the food, paused with a hand on her hip. "The king? Why?"

Their younger sister's eyes snapped to her. "Why not? If Alessia can meet the king, why shouldn't I?"

"Alessia is a contessa now, Fina," Liliana replied.

Serafina scowled. "So? I'm her sister. That should count for something."

Lilina snorted. "That's not how things work. Don't—"

"Oh, you wouldn't want to meet the king anyway, Serafina. Trust me," Dante cut in smoothly, "he's a total bore." He winked at her.

Serafina grinned, pushing her auburn curls over her shoulder. "I'd still like to make up my own mind about that. I heard he's a terrible cheat at cards."

Pamina nearly dropped the carafe of caffé she'd been carrying. "You shouldn't speak of the king like that, Fina. It's not... proper."

They all turned to look at her as if she had two heads. Heat spread across Pamina's face. If only Alessia were there to back her up. As much as Pamina loved her family, their blunt and coarse manner embarrassed her at times.

She tried to imagine how Stefano would respond had he been there to witness it all. Would he be able to accept her and her family just as Massimo and Dante had? Would he accept her?

Her chest tightened. No, she didn't think so.

Chapter 2

A New Start

Lorenzo

Lorenzo Bartoli stood in the middle of *Covelli's Bakery,* taking in the scenery around him. Sunlight streamed in from the giant storefront windows. Old wooden tables and chairs were set close together at the entrance. Behind him, the glass displays on the marble counter were empty and clean though there was still a faint smell of the sugary treats they'd once held. A shiny brass espresso machine stood in the corner behind the counter, looking much too modern and fancy for the little shop.

So, this is what their *father* had abandoned them for?

Lorenzo's eyebrows narrowed at the thought of the man. He glanced around some more, waiting for some kind of revelation or spark of something to hit him. Some kind of warmth or connection to the man who had sired him and his sister and then fled.

Instead, all he felt was anger. The sudden urge to toss over the tables and chairs filled him. He wanted to throw that expensive-looking espresso machine against the wall and watch it break into pieces.

11

He wouldn't, of course. Mainly because he wouldn't be able to sell it then. That and it would only prove what everyone falsely believed about goblins. That they were hot-tempered and violent. Prone to hysterics.

The image of his late mother, a full-blooded goblin, flashed before him, making his chest tighten. She'd been the gentlest, most level-headed person he'd ever known. Graceful and hard-working. Remembering her and the past only made his anger for his so-called father grow.

"Oh, Lor! Come have a look at this," came his sister's cheery voice, pulling him out of his dark thoughts.

Lorenzo turned, his gaze pausing on the oak wood floor beneath him. The sunlight highlighted the dust and dirt that had gathered there. The shop needed a good sweep and a fresh coat of polish. He sighed. All he wanted to do was take inventory, sell everything all together or piece by piece, and be done with it.

"What are you doing?" Giulia asked, joining him from the back room.

Lorenzo looked up and met his sister's gaze. She frowned, concern shining in her brown eyes as she stood, one hand on her hip. It was a look that was distinctly Mother and it made his throat constrict.

Shaking off the emotions, he sniffed. "Making note of everything. Just as you are supposed to be doing," he said, giving her a pointed look.

She waved his comment off. "Yes. Yes. But you should come and see what I found first."

Excitement flashed on her face, a stray black curl bobbing as she flounced toward him. Her boots thumped loudly against the wood as she closed the distance between them.

"Come on," she urged, grabbing him by the arm.

Lorenzo bit back a smile. There was the little sister he

knew. At almost twenty and one, Giulia was more a woman now than a girl. A fact that both made him proud and filled him with distress.

How much longer until she left him too?

"Now, I know you don't hold any affection for our father, Lor, but I think this might soften your heart," Giulia said carefully as she led him through the little kitchen and to the bedroom.

They stepped through the doorway and Lorenzo fought the urge to turn right back around. He didn't want to see the place the old man had called home.

The smell of candlewax and cinnamon filled the room along with the ashy scent coming from the fireplace. A cold draft came from the window near the bed.

It was a simple, sparsely furnished room and revealed nothing of who their father had been.

Lorenzo turned to his sister. "What exactly am I supposed to be looking at?"

She released his arm and stepped further into the room. "This. Come and look."

He watched as she grabbed a picture frame from the little side table. Turning back to him, she held it out for him.

It was a portrait of their mother when she was young. Her dark curls were piled high on her head, in a similar fashion to Giulia's, revealing pointed ears. She sat on a fancy chair, back straight and her chin lifted. Her lips quirked into a gentle smile.

The image was striking and nearly accurate. The artist had painted their mother's olive-green skin a shade darker, and her brown eyes wider and slightly more apart than they had been.

"He really did love her," Giulia spoke, making Lorenzo's head snap up.

A harsh laugh escaped him. "Love?"

He set the picture back on the side table.

Giulia's face hardened. "Yes. Love. I believe he did love her, and he probably regretted leaving us every day."

Lorenzo bit back the retort on his tongue. His sister was young and naïve. If she wanted to believe in a fairytale, who was he to stop her? Just because he didn't believe in love anymore, didn't mean she couldn't.

"We should have been here for the funeral, brother," Giulia added, regret flashing across her face.

Lorenzo snorted.

Her eyes narrowed at him. "At least we should have paid for the gravestone. We have more than enough to cover the expense."

"I will speak to the count and reimburse him, of course. Though I hate to think of any of our hard-earned money going to pay for the man who abandoned us. Abandoned mother."

Giulia gave him a pained look that cut right through him.

"He's gone now. Can't you let your bitterness die with him? Mother would not approve of your cruelty, Lor."

"Yet she accepted his," he muttered.

The anguished expression on his sister's face made him instantly regret his words. He reached a hand out to her and she took it, tears welling in her eyes.

"Mother always wanted you to forgive him. If you can't do that, can't you forget him? Seeing you carrying this grudge for so long... it's not healthy, Lor."

Forgive. Forget. The two things his mother and sister wanted him to do were the two things he simply couldn't. He didn't understand how they could. The bastard had left them and for that, Lorenzo could never forgive him.

That wasn't what his sister wanted to hear though, and as much as he hated his *father,* he loved his sister more.

"I'm trying," he answered softly.

He wasn't. But the hopeful smile Giulia gave him was

worth the little lie. She'd been through enough heartache the past year. First, they lost their mother to sickness, then Giulia's broken engagement, and now their *father* was gone. Lorenzo would do whatever he could to help her heal.

Giulia shivered as she let go of his hand. She turned to look back at the picture of their mother and sighed. "I miss her so much."

A lump grew in Lorenzo's throat.

With her back to him now and her black curls piled delicately atop her head, she looked just like their mother. Thinking of his mother, the woman his father had abandoned to start a new life, made him seethe once more.

He wouldn't let that happen to Giulia. It was the reason he had been forced to break off her engagement, though she didn't know it. She thought it was her betrothed's idea, but Lorenzo had gone behind her back and pressed the man's family to call off the engagement.

She trusts you and you've lied to her. A tiny voice in his head spoke.

It's for the best, he argued back.

Though the man she claimed to love seemed genuine, his family hadn't approved of the match. They were only more than happy to help Lorenzo with the scheme of breaking it off. Giulia was half-goblin. Eventually, the man would have agreed with his family and where would that have left his sister?

"When are we returning home?" Giulia asked.

Her question caught him off guard.

She turned to him and met his gaze. Guilt prickled at him at her earnest look. He hadn't told her yet, but they wouldn't be going back to the city. They couldn't go back to the city. Not until she was over her broken engagement. He couldn't risk her going back to that man.

"Lor?" she asked, frowning.

He cleared his throat and forced himself to hold her stare. "I have a surprise for you. I've booked us a trip. After we've finished selling the bakery and tying up some loose ends, we're sailing for the Regno Unito."

Giulia's eyes widened. She gasped and threw herself at him, squeezing him tight. "Oh! You are the best brother in the world!"

Her words cut through him like a knife. It was his sister's dream trip, one he'd been promising her for a while. It would be far away from Riccardo Davici, the man who'd claimed her heart. In time, she would forget about him. Lorenzo would make sure of it.

She released him and stepped back with a hesitant look. "Oh, but, Lor, we can't sell the bakery."

Lorenzo felt his eyebrows shoot up. "Of course, we can. We must. You know we came here to do just that, Giulia."

She bit her lip, eyes darting away. "I know that's what we came here to do, but it would be wrong."

"Wrong? How would it be wrong?"

Giulia took a deep breath and released it. "We can't sell our father's bakery."

Lorenzo scoffed. "Why not? If it's a bakery you want, we can sell this and buy a different one. A better one. A bigger one. This one is hardly much of a bakery anyway."

Giulia frowned. "I don't want a different one. I want this one. It was left for us, Lor. If you don't want it, I'll buy your share. You'll have your half of whatever it would have sold for."

"Don't be ridiculous, Giulia, you can't possibly mean to keep it. You don't know the first thing about running a bakery."

She huffed, arms crossed over her chest. "So? I can hire some help. It can't be that hard. I don't need your permission to do this."

Lorenzo gaped at her. He hadn't expected this. His sister

wanting to keep and run the bakery was not part of his carefully worked out plan.

"You can't possibly be serious. Do you know how much work and time this would take? And this town. They don't even have a proper modiste! You'd give everything up for this? You'd give up the Regno Unito?"

Her look of determination wavered. Then she lifted her chin. "Of course, I don't want to give up the trip. You know I've wanted to go there since I was little, but, this is important. It's our inheritance. I understand if you don't want it, Lor, but you never asked if I did. And I do. I want to keep it."

"Oh, Giulia," Lorenzo said with a shake of his head.

He could tell there would be no changing her mind. There never was once it was made up, but he also knew the lavish life-style and travel his sister loved would change her mind in the end. Giulia was a city girl, through and through. Once she realized how boring and mundane the little mountain town was, she'd give up this silly notion and move on.

Perhaps, it would give her more time to forget about her broken engagement.

"You won't change my mind about this," Giulia said, arms still crossed in front of her.

Lorenzo sighed and nodded. "I know. I guess I can always exchange our tickets for a later date."

A smile flashed on her face. "Does that mean you'll stay too?"

"Of course. I can't leave you here to set up shop all by yourself. What kind of brother would I be?"

Giulia squealed delightedly and threw her arms around him. "Oh, it's going to be great! We've never owned a bakery before."

A snort escaped him. "Yes, which brings the question, who is going to do all the baking?"

Releasing him, his sister held a finger up to her chin in thought. "Surely, our father had employees. He couldn't have possibly done it all by himself."

Lorenzo bit back the admonishment on his tongue. He wished Giulia would stop referring to the scoundrel as father. Though the thought of the man running the bakery on his own with no help filled Lorenzo with a little satisfaction.

He'd chosen to leave them. Chosen to be alone. It only served him right that he died with no family to mourn him. They'd spent enough of their lifetime mourning him.

Lorenzo was glad he was gone. The harsh thought startled him. Pushing it away, he took a deep breath. The cold autumn air swirled against the window, whistling loudly and pulling him from his thoughts.

Perhaps, his sister was right. Perhaps it was time to finally let go of the past. Though the last thing he wanted was to spend more time at the bakery his father had loved more than them, maybe it would help him to set aside the bitterness he'd been harboring all these years.

Yes. Maybe it was time for a fresh start for both him and Giulia.

Chapter 3

The Heirs

Pamina

"Good evening, neighbors!" Salvatore Rossi's cheerful voice called from the front door of his villa. Adriano, his giant faun husband, stood beside him.

Mama waved in greeting. Pamina followed her and her sisters up the stone path, making sure to close the wooden gate behind them. The sky was beginning to darken overhead and a heavy gust of wind blew through the trees, shaking the branches. She would be glad to get inside and sit by the fire.

Horses neighed from the stable as they passed by, drawing Serafina's attention.

She frowned. "The horses want more hay," she whispered to Pamina.

Pamina gave her a warning glance. Serafina's magic was not something their neighbors nor anyone outside their family knew about. She could talk to animals and make them do her bidding. Even with Massimo, a half-fae, becoming the new count, the people of Zamerra were still suspicious of magic. They didn't know of Fiorella's plant and earth magic either.

Liliana's tonics and Pamina's enchanted pastries were hard

enough for them to accept, but the magic of the younger girls would cause too much fear and chaos.

Mama glanced back at them. "I'll mention it to our hosts. Come along, girls. Mind your manners."

Pamina brought up the rear, ushering her younger sisters forward. Alessia and Massimo's wagon was already parked outside the stable along with Dante and Liliana's. For a minute, Pamina paused, wondering what it would be like to arrive at a dinner party with her own man in their own wagon.

"Oh! Alessia and Massimo are already here," Fiorella shouted, startling her out of her thoughts.

"Ugh. And so is Angelo," Serafina added, pointing at the third empty cart.

No wonder the horses wanted more hay. There were extra mouths that night in the stable.

Mama's head snapped to Serafina. "The Rossi's have always been generous and kind with us. I expect you to show them the same courtesy, Serafina."

Pamina felt her mouth drop at her mother's firm tone. Serafina and Fiorella looked just as shocked. Serafina rarely got scolded by their mother, though her sharp tongue often warranted it.

Instead of arguing with Mama as she usually did, Serafina wisely kept her mouth shut. Though her face was stormy with anger.

Pamina gripped the tray in her hands tighter. It was a good thing she'd brought her enchanted cannoli. Her sister's favorite. They were filled with delicious ricotta and a calming, content-ment spell. The magic was temporary, but it would help soothe her sister's emotions.

"And if Signora Rossi is here tonight, I hope you will show her the same courtesy you expect from us as well," Serafina said under her breath.

Fiorella's eyes bugged. Pamina gasped. It was no secret that their mother didn't get along with Salvatore and Angelo's mother, Signora Rossi. Even Pamina had little nice to say about the cantankerous woman.

Mama paused halfway on the path and fixed Serafina with a warning look. "Enough."

With that, she turned and pasted on a smile for their neighbors. "Signores! Thank you for having us."

Pamina glanced at Serafina, whose lip curled defiantly. *Santo Cielo.* She hoped her sister wouldn't cause any trouble at the dinner.

"Signorinas, welcome!" Salvatore Rossi greeted them warmly. He took the tray from Pamina, brown eyes gleaming.

Adriano smiled politely and ushered them inside. Pamina smiled back as she entered their villa. Warmth enveloped her, the smell of burning logs and something savory filling her nose. It wasn't her recipe, but it would still taste delicious. Food, even ordinary, had its own magic.

Stepping forward, Adriano offered to take their coats. His hooves clomped against the wooden floor as he walked the heavy coats to the rack, the noise filling the silence.

Pamina caught Fiorella staring at the bottom of Adriano's long pants. No doubt trying to catch a glimpse of his hooves.

"Ella," Pamina said, nudging her sister forward.

Fiorella's eyes snapped to her, a sheepish look on her face. The Rossis, like the Silveris, were somewhat of outcasts in Zamerra. They lived up the mountain next to the Silveris and mostly kept to themselves.

Salvatore led them through the front entrance and into the sitting room. Fire roared from a finely carved stone fireplace in the back of the room. Candles were lit along the wall and in the holders on the side tables, casting a golden glow that highlighted the oil paintings and fancy décor.

Voices stopped and heads turned as they arrived. Salvatore's younger brother, Angelo, sat on a chair next to Liliana and Dante, the rest of the Rossi family missing. Alessia and Massimo were seated on a delicately embroidered loveseat. Alessia rose to greet them first.

"Massimo!" Fiorella said, hurrying past their sister to greet the fae.

He smiled, returning her fierce hug. "Hello, Ella."

Alessia gave a mocking huff. "Well, where's my hug, Ella?"

Pamina smiled as she watched her sisters hug, waiting for her turn. Though Alessia and Massimo lived close by, she missed having her oldest sister in the villa with them. Alessia, unlike the rest of them, didn't have magic, but she was the only one who could hear their enchanted villa speak.

"Pamina!" Alessia greeted, pulling her into a tight embrace.

She smelled like roses and candlewax. Her dark curls were loose, tickling Pamina's face as she squeezed her.

Liliana snorted behind them. "You'd think you had been gone a whole year and not just two weeks."

Alessia released Pamina and turned to give Liliana a hug too. "Two weeks away from Zamerra is too long. We're happy to be home."

Massimo nodded in agreement. "Very happy."

"Where's Lucia?" Serafina, who'd been ignoring Angelo's attempt to greet her, spoke up.

Massimo and Alessia shared a look.

"You do know your cat is welcome anytime," Salvatore, their host, said with a quick glance at his husband.

"Of course. Thank you. I'm afraid this weather doesn't agree with her. She prefers to stay indoors and besides, after our recent trip, I don't think she'll be ready to travel again for quite some time," Massimo said, fire reflected in his amber eyes.

Alessia smirked. "No, I don't think so. Cats and carriages don't get along very well."

Dante huffed. "Didn't the sleeping lotion we gave you work?"

Massimo turned to his friend with an embarrassed smile. "Well, yes, quite well, actually. Just not on Lucia. You see, I accidentally spilled it."

"Yes. All over himself. He slept the whole three hours," Alessia added, giving her husband an affectionate smile.

Chuckles and teasing followed, but Massimo was too lost in his wife's stare to hear them. Once more, Pamina felt a tightness in her chest. Salvatore had Adriano. Alessia had Massimo, Liliana had Dante, and everyone knew Angelo was smitten with Serafina. Watching the couples around her made her acutely aware of her own singleness.

Did she have a match somewhere out there?

Salvatore cleared his throat, getting all their attention. "I'm just going to put this delicious tray in the kitchen," his gaze flicked to Pamina. "Everyone, take a seat, please. The dinner should be ready soon. Enjoy the appetizers for now."

Adriano waved a hand around the lavishly decorated sitting room as Salvatore disappeared to the kitchen. Pamina took a seat next to her mother, pushing herself into the corner to make space.

The others sat too, voices murmuring together. Alessia and Massimo divulged them with stories from their recent trip, but Pamina's mind was elsewhere.

She was happy, truly happy, for her sisters, but she couldn't help but feel a twinge of envy. Grabbing an olive from the tray of antipasto in front of her, Pamina said a quick, silent chant over it before popping it into her mouth.

Right away, she felt lighter. She didn't like to use her magic on herself like that, but she didn't know how else she was going to get through the dinner. She couldn't let her gloomy mood ruin the party.

Mama stiffened beside her, casting her a sharp glance. Pamina shook her head slightly to let her know she wouldn't cast again. Mama's dark eyes drilled into her, a knowing look on her face. Pamina fought the urge to squirm under her stare. She hadn't meant to draw attention to herself.

"Are you well, *amore?* You're not coming down with something, are you?" Mama whispered.

Pamina shook her head. "No, Mama. I'm fine."

Her mother didn't look convinced, but she dropped the subject.

Salvatore returned to the room and addressed them. "I hope I didn't miss any delicious gossip. What I want to know about are Signor Covelli's heirs. Has anyone here met them yet?"

"Heirs? He has more than one heir?" Pamina asked, unable to hide her surprise.

Salvatore nodded and continued. "I've also heard they're not... I mean, they have... well, they're green."

"You mean they're goblins?" Fiorella blurted, her green eyes widening.

Salvatore shrugged and looked to Massimo for an explanation. Everyone followed his gaze. Massimo, who didn't like to be the center of attention, flushed, the tips of his pointed fae ears turning red.

"Yes, it seems Signor Covelli left his bakery to a son and a daughter. While they didn't disclose their heritage to me, they are... well, as you put it, green. They go by their mother's name however. Bartoli," Massimo finally answered.

Dante scoffed. "Has no one here met a goblin before? Massimo, I know you have."

"We've never had a goblin in Zamerra before. Let alone two," Serafina said, face growing excited.

"They only just arrived yesterday. I ran into Signor Bartloli as he was preparing his wagon to leave for the inn," Dante continued.

Salvatore's gaze snapped to him. "They're staying at the Blossom Inn? Not at the bakery?"

Dante shrugged. "It appears so."

"How curious," Salvatore said, rubbing his chin in thought.

Adriano sighed and laid a hand on his husband's shoulder. "Oh no, you don't."

"What?" Salvatore frowned.

The faun shook his head. "I know that look. Don't go sticking your nose into their business, *amore*. At least not until they've settled in. They're still in mourning."

Dante snorted. "I don't think you'll get much information, anyway. He wasn't a very chatty man."

Liliana clucked her tongue at her fiancé. "Well, you hardly give anyone a chance to get a word in."

He gave her an affronted look. "I like to make small talk. What's wrong with that?"

"Speaking of small talk... I heard they plan to keep the bakery. Run it themselves. They're looking to hire a baker," Salvatore said, catching Pamina's eyes.

"Oh. Well, I'm sure they'll keep on Signora Bianchi," Pamina answered, her face heating as everyone looked at her.

"If they're smart, they'll sack her immediately," Serafina said.

"Fina! What an awful thing to say," Pamina scolded her.

Her sister shrugged. "Well, she can't bake. Someone should tell them before they make the mistake of keeping her on."

Mama grunted and turned her attention to Pamina. "Perhaps you should offer your service, *amore*."

"Yes, you're the best baker in town," Alessia agreed.

Fiorella nodded. "Ooh, I can help too!"

Liliana frowned at her. "Ella, you have enough work helping Mama in the garden."

She exchanged a look with Alessia. Pamina knew what they were thinking. Fiorella's plant magic was powerful and uncontrollable at times. Even with the use of her enchanted gloves, it was risky to let her touch anything edible. There was no telling what kind of magic would leak out.

Fiorella shrank into her seat. The disappointed look on her face twisted Pamina's heart.

Signora Sanchez, the Rossi's cook, appeared in the doorway and cleared her throat. "Dinner is ready, Signores."

"Thank you," Salvatore answered with a nod.

He turned to the room. "Shall we?"

Mama stood first, taking Salvatore's arm and everyone else followed. Pamina took Adriano's arm and glanced back to see Angelo offer his to Serafina and Fiorella.

Serafina's freckled nose wrinkled as she accepted it, but thankfully, she kept her rude comments to herself. Serafina and Angelo had been schoolmates when they were younger. Before Serafina was expelled indefinitely for bringing snakes into the school house. Snakes that had 'mysteriously' ended up in poor Angelo's trousers.

Though her sister wouldn't admit it, Pamina had long suspected there was something more to their childish rivalry and pranks. Something that looked a lot like what Alessia and Liliana had found.

Would she ever find it herself?

"Are you well, Signorina?" Adriano's deep voice startled her.

Pamina nodded and looked up at him. "Yes, I'm sorry. Just lost in my thoughts."

The faun frowned. "No need to be sorry. I know you were fond of Signor Covelli. He was a kind man. Always made me feel welcome in his bakery, and well, you know, there aren't that many places in Zamerra where someone like me is welcomed."

His words made Pamina sad. Though she knew what it was like to be an outcast and a target of gossip because of her size and her family, she didn't face the same discrimination as Adriano did for his hooves. Why were people so quick to judge others?

"You should be welcomed anywhere in Zamerra. I'm sorry anyone has made you feel otherwise."

Adriano shrugged off her words as he led her into the dining room. Pamina withdrew her hand from his arm and smoothed out her skirt as Adriano stepped forward to pull out a chair for her.

"This looks delicious," Pamina said, taking her seat.

Mama nodded beside her. "Yes. Thank you for having us."

Everyone else murmured their appreciation. Signora Sanchez had outdone herself with the dinner. Fancy porcelain dishes were filled with various steaming pasta and vegetables. At the far end of the table, there was a giant bowl of tortellini soup with beef that filled the room with its savory smell.

Pamina sighed. Though she was thankful for the food and time with her family and friends, she couldn't help but feel that something was missing. *A someone.* She shook away the thought and forced a smile.

She had her mother and sisters, and now Massimo and Dante. They had their dear neighbors. Why couldn't this be enough for her?

Chapter 4

The Offer

Lorenzo

L orenzo swallowed down the last of his lukewarm caffé and set down his mug on the kitchen table. The older woman sitting across from him watched him with a furrowed brow.

They'd only been in Zamerra for three days and it was clear, none of the townsfolk they'd run into had ever seen a half-goblin before. Another good reason for them to sell the bakery and go back to the city. It was much easier to blend in there.

"More caffé, Signora Bianchi?" Giulia asked, standing to get the carafe.

The woman blinked, looking away from Giulia's ears. "No. Thank you."

They fell into silence. The sound of wagon wheels and horse hooves echoed outside the bakery along with the morning calls from the people starting their day.

Signora Bianchi cleared her throat and glanced at the door behind her. "I do appreciate your offer, but truth be told, I'm ready to hang up my apron."

Her gaze flicked to Lorenzo. "I probably should have done it ages ago. My hands aren't as steady as they used to be. Your... Signor Covelli was kind enough to keep me on all these years," she said with a sniff.

Pausing to wipe her eyes with a handkerchief, she shook her head at Lorenzo. "Kind man, your father."

Lorenzo scoffed. Giulia nudged him with an elbow in warning.

Before he could say more, his sister stood and clapped her hands together. "Yes. Well, we don't want to keep you too long, Signora. Thank you for coming in to speak to us."

The older woman nodded. "Of course, Signorina. I owe your father that much."

Her eyes snagged on Giulia's pointed ears before dancing away.

"Oh. One last question, Signora Bianchi. Do you know of any other bakers or helpers my father employed here? Anyone else with his skill and knowledge?"

"Well, sometimes he hired a few extra hands for large events, but I wouldn't call them *skilled* hands," Signora Bianchi said with a raised brow.

She leaned back in her chair and frowned. "There is one girl who helped us from time to time who showed promise. A lot of promise, actually."

Giulia's face lit up with excitement. "Oh? Does she still live here? What is her name?"

Signora Bianchi grunted. "She lives up the mountain with her mother and sisters. Pamina Silveri is her name, but I should warn you, Signorina, her family has quite the reputation."

Lorenzo shared a curious look with his sister.

"Pamina is the third of five daughters. No fathers. And it's a known fact that they practice magic. Her mother is a seer! In fact, the second oldest, Liliana, is your next-door neighbor. She runs that *apothecary*."

The older woman's face flushed, spittle flying as she talked.

"Oh, yes. You've met her fiancé, Lor. Signor Lazzaro, wasn't it?" Giulia turned to him with a pointed look.

It was time for the rambling woman to leave.

Signora Bianchi grunted again and leaned forward. "He's a warlock. Not a pharmacist. I did warn your father about him. I—"

Lorenzo stood and offered the woman an arm up. "Yes, well, thank you for your concern, Signora Bianchi. Would you like me to get the wagon and drive you back home?"

Signora Bianchi's eyes widened at Lorenzo's arm. She quickly stood and turned away. "Oh. No. That won't be necessary. Thank you. I'm only a few steps from home."

Though he had a feeling she didn't want to be seen with them, he didn't mind the refusal. He had better things to do than drive the woman around town.

"Good day, Signora," Giulia added, rising to her feet.

The woman nodded at her and saw herself out the door. Her boots echoed against the wooden floor as she crossed the front of the shop. She slammed the front door shut behind her.

"She moves pretty quickly for her age," Lorenzo said, throwing Giulia an amused smile.

His sister frowned, arms crossed in front of her. "She was rude. Acting as if she didn't see your arm there."

Lorenzo shrugged. "This is a small town. They've probably never seen our like before. Are you sure you still want to do this?"

Determination flashed in Giulia's eyes. "Of course."

He sighed. "Then I suppose we should finish taking inventory and seeing about hiring some help."

Giulia tucked a curl behind her ear and frowned. "Did you hear that?"

A gentle knock sounded from the front door. Lorenzo bit

back a groan. They had much to do and the last thing he wanted was to entertain anyone.

Giulia hurried past him to the front of the shop, her fancy dress billowing out behind her. It wasn't a sensible outfit for the bakery, but Lorenzo had learned not to comment on his sister's choice of fashion. Not unless he wanted a verbal lashing.

"Wait for me," Lorenzo said, catching up to her.

He made it to the door just as his sister opened it. Cold air swirled in, bringing in the smell of smoke and autumn.

A group of people, mostly women, stood before them. Lorenzo recognized the two men in their company. Their neighbor, Signor Lazzaro, who ran the apothecary and Count Gallo, the half-fae count of Zamerra.

Count Gallo stepped forward. "Good morning, Signor Bartoli. Signorina. I hope we're not disturbing you."

Lorenzo grunted. "We're quite busy actually. There's much to do."

"Oh. My apologies, Signor Bartoli. I ..." The man trailed off, glancing at the woman beside him. His face reddened, the color spreading to the tips of his pointed ears. His clearly fae ears.

Giulia shot Lorenzo a dark look before stepping in front of him. "Oh, you must be Count Gallo!"

"Please come in," she added, opening the door wider and motioning them inside.

Lorenzo bit back a sigh as he stepped aside to give them room. He'd met the count already when he'd reimbursed him for the gravestone. What did he want now?

He watched as the group followed the count into the bakery. Signor Lazzaro, their neighbor, nodded at him from the back. Who were all these women they'd brought with them?

"Thank you. This is my wife, Contessa Gallo," the count said, motioning one of the young women forward.

Her dark eyes flitted to them. "You can just call me Signora Gallo. It's a pleasure to meet you, Signor. Signorina."

She glanced at the older woman beside her, who had the same bronze complexion and dark curls. "This is my mother, Signora Silveri."

Giulia shot Lorenzo a look. It was the seer Signora Bianchi had told them about.

"Nice to meet you, Signora Silveri," Giulia said with a smile.

"You as well, Signorina. Signor." The woman smiled back, shrewd eyes darting from his sister to him.

"These are my daughters. Liliana, Pamina, Serafina, and Fiorella," she said, waving a hand at each in turn.

Lorenzo's gaze snagged on Pamina. The one Signora Bianchi had told them about.

Her light brown eyes met his and a flush spread across her face. Mahogany curls contrasted with her light tan skin and her full, pink lips curved into a smile. She stood a little shorter than her mother and older sisters, her wool coat hugging her generous curves.

She was stunning.

Realizing he was staring, Lorenzo tore his gaze away and nodded politely. "A pleasure to meet you, Signorinas."

They returned his greeting in unison.

"Yes, and we've already met, Signor. It's nice to make your acquaintance though, Signorina," Signor Lazzaro said with a nod in Giulia's direction.

Giulia smiled. "Yes. A pleasure, Signor. I've been wanting to stop in next door and have a look around."

The man smiled. "You're welcome any time."

Lorenzo fought back a wave of frustration. They didn't have time for niceties. He didn't want to be rude, but he had much to do, and entertaining these people was not on his list.

Giulia glanced at him, eyebrow arched in warning. "My brother and I were just discussing you, Signorina."

She turned her gaze to Pamina. The young woman's eyes widened, her lips slightly parting in surprise.

"Me?" she squeaked out.

She tugged at the bottom of her coat, the movement drawing Lorenzo's eye. He averted his gaze, trying to regain his composure. Her nervousness was endearing, but Lorenzo didn't need the distraction. And Pamina Silveri was definitely a distraction.

"Yes. Signora Bianchi told us you were the most promising baker in town," Giulia continued excitedly.

One of the younger girls snorted. "Promising? Pamina is the best baker in Zamerra. Much better than Signora Bianchi. Did you just sack the old woman? We saw her leaving here in a hurry," she said brightly.

"Fina!" Her sister shot her a look, face reddening even further. She turned back to face Giulia. "Forgive my sister's bluntness. That was kind of the Signora to say. I do love baking. Your father was an excellent baker. I'm so sorry for your loss."

The sorrowful look on her face seemed sincere. Signora Bianchi said the young woman had helped the old man in the bakery many times. Had she formed a connection with him?

The idea that their father had been more of a father to Pamina Silveri than his own daughter filled Lorenzo with anger.

"Yes. Thank you," Giulia answered, giving Lorenzo another warning look.

She turned her attention back to the young woman. "We'd love to hire you, Signorina Silveri. With your help and guidance, we'd love to keep the bakery running."

Lorenzo watched the woman's reaction as his sister chattered on. Surprise and curiosity shone in her eyes. Her gaze met his.

Heat spread through him at her stare. If she agreed to this arrangement, he would need to keep his distance. It was clear his body, traitor that it was, was drawn to her. The last thing he needed was a distraction in the form of a beautiful woman.

"I'd be happy to help you. I can bring some of my own recipes too, if you like," Pamina Silveri said, eyes darting away shyly.

Giulia clapped her hands together. "Oh, that would be lovely! Yes, please. We'll pay you of course. When can you start? Can you start today?"

"Today?" Lorenzo and Pamina spoke at the same time.

He glared at his sister. Why was she rushing into this?

"Giulia, we haven't even finished inventory," Lorenzo said with a shake of his head.

He turned to Pamina. "Perhaps tomorrow?"

She looked from him to Giulia and nodded. "Of course, Signor. Whatever you need."

Giulia shrugged. "We would invite you all to stay for caffé, but I'm afraid my brother hasn't learned how to run the espresso machine yet."

Lorenzo gave her a flat look she pretended not to notice.

"Oh, Pamina can run the machine. Can't you?" Signora Silveri spoke up, nudging her daughter forward.

"Mama. I... I could try. I'm not sure I remember all the steps, though," Pamina stuttered.

Lorenzo didn't like the calculating look in the older woman's gaze. Didn't she realize they were half-goblins? Or perhaps the Silveri's reputation was so far tainted that a half-goblin son-in-law didn't matter to her. He glanced at the count and Signor Lazzaro. She'd already welcomed a half-fae and warlock into the family.

Unfortunately for them, Lorenzo wasn't on the market.

He'd proposed marriage before and it had led to nothing but heartache. He wouldn't make that mistake again.

"Why didn't you come for the funeral, Signor? Didn't you want to say goodbye?" the youngest girl asked, drawing everyone's attention.

One of her sisters gasped and Signora Silveri frowned at her, shaking her head gently.

Lorenzo exchanged a look with Giulia, who chose that moment to fall silent.

Lorenzo met the young girl's stare. "Because we... well, we didn't want to."

The girl's eyes widened. An awkward silence followed.

Giulia snorted. "*You* didn't want to," she muttered.

"But he was your father," the girl continued.

"Ella." Her mother stopped her.

"You can't ask those kind of questions, Ella. It's rude," her sister, Serafina, admonished her.

The young girl looked as if she wanted to disappear into the ground. Pamina wrapped an arm around her, giving Lorenzo and Giulia an embarrassed smile.

"That's alright. It's a valid question," Giulia answered kindly.

She glanced back at Lorenzo with a questioning look. He shook his head slightly. These people were strangers. They didn't need to know their whole story. It would only be a matter of time before the whole town was talking about them.

"Well, we should get back to the inventory. Thank you for coming in," Lorenzo said, hoping they'd get the hint.

Giulia frowned at him.

"Yes, of course. Thank you for your time. Please let me know if you need anything," Count Gallo said, nodding in earnest.

Everyone else murmured their replies as well, boots shuffling as they headed back out of the shop. Pamina paused in the doorway and turned to them.

"What time would you like me to come tomorrow?" she asked softly.

"In the afternoon," Lorenzo said just as Giulia responded, "First thing in the morning."

Pamina glanced between them with a look of uncertainty.

"First thing in the morning," Giulia repeated, ignoring Lorenzo's glare.

He turned to the young woman and sighed. "Well, the boss has spoken," he muttered.

Pamina gave him a tight smile as if she didn't know what to make of his comment. Before he could say more, she turned on her heel and followed the rest of the party outside. Across the cobblestone plaza, shopkeepers and passersby were gathered, watching.

They had an audience now.

Giulia waved goodbye and shut the door. Then she turned to Lorenzo with a scowl.

"What?" he asked.

She huffed. "Did you have to be so sour? You're going to scare her off."

Lorenzo grunted. "It's not my disposition that scares the ladies off, Giulia. One look at me and they tend to run the other way."

Giulia rolled her eyes at him. "That's not true, Lor."

She pursed her lips and tapped her chin. "I like her. What did you think?"

"I think we need to get started on inventory and get supplies. Otherwise, Signorina Silveri will have nothing to do when she comes *first thing in the morning*."

Giulia waved his words away and watched the Silveri

family leave from the shop window. Lorenzo didn't like the calculating look in his sister's eye.

This bakery scheme was getting less and less appealing. *Business.* It was just business, and the sooner it failed, the sooner he could convince his sister to move on.

Chapter 5

Changes

Pamina

P amina wrapped up her long curls before washing her hands in the kitchen sink. The icy water made her shiver. She quickly dried off with the cloth hanging from the wall. Early morning light streaked in from the window above the sink.

She stared out at their backyard and the forest in the distance. Fiorella's lavender had grown so tall that the flowers nearly blocked the view. Her sister had been trying, unsuccessfully, to get the plant to move further away from the villa, but the stubborn flowers refused to budge.

The fire roared to life in the hearth behind Pamina, making her jump. She glanced up at the wooden rafters.

Thank you, she said to the villa, though she didn't know if it could hear her.

With Alessia and Liliana moved out, the villa had grown more active, helping them with the morning routine.

Pamina stood by the fire, letting its warmth wash over her. The wood stack outside would need to be refilled soon and that was one task the villa couldn't do. Pamina made a note to check on it later.

Finally warm enough, Pamina turned away and walked over to sink to get started. She hummed as she opened the cupboard to retrieve the tin of caffé beans.

A shuffling sound came from the pantry. Pamina glanced back to see Bruno, their house elf, yawning as he trundled out of the storeroom.

"Good morning, Bruno," she greeted him.

The little elf grumbled something in Elvish and walked over to her. Pamina moved his stool from the table to the counter so he could hop up.

"I have to make the caffé first, Bruno. Then I'll start on breakfast," she told him as he scrambled up the stool.

His bushy brows furrowed at her. With a grunt, he pulled himself up to the counter and scratched his wiry beard. Bruno watched as she scooped the fresh beans into the grinder and started cranking.

"Pamina? You're still here, *amore?*" Mama's voice sounded from the doorway.

Pamina turned to her. "Good morning, Mama. How are you feeling today? No headaches, I hope?"

Mama leaned over to blow out the candle on the table and looked up to meet her gaze. "No. Why do you ask?"

Pamina shrugged, turning back around to finish grinding the caffé. The strong smell wafted in the room and the crunching sound filled the silence.

Mama sighed and walked over to her. "Pamina, if I had a vision, I would tell you, *amore*. Especially if it concerned you. You know I can't control what I see or force it."

"I know, Mama," Pamina replied, plastering on a smile as she turned to her mother.

Mama searched her face, a knowing look in her brown eyes. "Is this about Signor Bartoli?"

Heat spread up Pamina's neck. "What? No! I just met the man. I know nothing about him."

Mama shrugged and wrapped her robe tighter around herself. "Well, that's an easy remedy. I'm sure you'll get to know him better after today."

A sly grin spread on her mother's face. Bruno, who'd been patiently waiting for his caffé, stomped his little slipper on the counter and motioned for Pamina to finish.

Pamina took the copper percolator from the cupboard and removed the inner basket before filling the bottom with water. Then she scooped the grounds into the basket before placing it back into the percolator. She carried it to the hearth. Mama hurried over to move the grate on top of the flames for her.

Mama fell silent as Pamina set the caffé maker down on the grate and stepped back. Pamina raised her hands toward it and closed her eyes, letting the magic wash over her.

Energy. Strength. Stamina.

She envisioned each as a little thread and carefully wove them together before directing her spell to the fire. She felt her own strength and energy falter as the spell took.

Mama laid a hand on her shoulder, startling her. Pamina met her shrewd gaze.

"Your time will come, Pamina. I truly believe that."

Warmth surged through her at her mother's words. She hoped Mama was right.

"You should get going, *amore*," Mama said, giving her a kiss on the head.

"You're leaving already? Can I come too?" Fiorella's hopeful voice came from the doorway.

Mama shook her head no. "Not today, Ella. I need your

help in the garden. We have much to do before the Harvest Festival."

Pamina shot her sister an apologetic smile. Fiorella frowned, pushing her long, chestnut braid behind her thin shoulder. Her green eyes grew watery as she looked at Pamina.

"Ella, what is it?" Pamina hurried to her.

Fiorella blinked back her tears. "First Alessia left and then Liliana. Are you going to leave too, Pamina?"

Pamina pulled her into a tight hug, her sister's words stinging her. "Of course not, Ella. I'm just helping in the bakery. I'll be back later."

Fiorella shook her head against her. "No. That's not what I mean. Everyone is leaving. Even Serafina said she's going to leave someday. And I'll be left here all alone!"

Pamina frowned. Serafina wanted to leave Zamerra? That was a surprise. Out of all them, Serafina had always seemed to have the greatest attachment to the little town.

Mama walked over and gently extracted Fiorella from Pamina's embrace. "I know these changes are hard, *amore,* but that is how life goes. Besides, Alessia and Liliana haven't gone far. We're lucky for the time that we've had all together and if Serafina wants to leave someday, we will still be family. It's going to be okay."

Fiorella nestled her face against Mama's chest and sniffed. "I wish we could freeze time and keep things how they are forever."

Mama laughed and exchanged a look with Pamina. "But then you would miss out on all the good things to come, Ella."

Bruno, who'd been watching the scene, hopped off the counter to the stool and then to the ground. He scurried over to Fiorella and tugged at the bottom of her night dress.

She released Mama and knelt down beside him to give him

a kiss on his pointed red hat. He shouted something in Elvish and held out a tiny hand to her.

"What is it, Bruno?" Fiorella asked, placing a finger into his outstretched hand.

"*Noss'e per sempre,*" he said with an earnest look.

"He said family forever," Serafina answered, appearing in the kitchen.

Her eyebrow arched at them curiously, her auburn curls spilling out of her braid. "What is going on in here?"

"You said you were going to leave Zamerra, Fina," Fiorella said with an accusing tone.

Serafina rolled her eyes. "Yes, but it's not like I'm leaving today. And it wouldn't be forever. I just want to see other places for a change. Besides, you can always come with me."

Fiorella's face brightened at this. "Oooh! Could we go to the Youngfrou Forest? We could bring another plant like Tito home."

Pamina fought the urge to shudder. Tito was Fiorella's giant carnivorous plant that Dante had gifted her. Though it had learned to only feed on insects and the table food Fiorella fed it, the outdoor cats and their little dog, Gio, gave it a wide berth in the yard.

"Yes, well. The Youngfrou forest will have to wait for another day, *amores*. Today, we need to look over the vegetables for the Harvest Festival," Mama said with an amused smile.

Guilt prickled Pamina's skin. "Oh, Mama. I'll be home as soon as I can to help."

Mama frowned. "We can handle it, Pamina. You should get going. Serafina, go help her get Fabrizio hitched."

Serafina huffed. "I haven't even fed him yet."

"It's fine, Mama. The walk sounds nice, anyway. It will warm me up," Pamina said, trying to keep the peace.

The percolator gurgled behind them, filling the silence.

Pamina grabbed a cloth before removing it from the fire. She set it on the kitchen counter and moved the ceramic carafe closer. The rich smell of the caffé filled her nose as she poured it into the enchanted carafe. It would keep the liquid warm until the enchantment wore off.

"Here. At least take something to eat on the way," Mama said, tucking two wrapped croissants into the pocket of Pamina's skirt.

"Thank you. I'll start supper as soon as I get back," Pamina replied, pouring herself a cup of caffé.

She stirred in a large spoonful of sugar and held the mug up to her face, breathing in the rich aroma. After blowing a few times, she took a tentative sip. The smooth liquid filled her with warmth and a burst of energy.

The spell spread through her, making her feel bright and ready to start the day.

Bruno hurried over and grabbed his little mug from the corner of the counter. Pamina smiled at him as she poured some for him before finishing off her own mug.

After grabbing her coat from the rack, she wrapped it around herself and said goodbye to her family. Then she laced up her boots and opened the back door. Cold blasted her face as she stepped out.

The sun had risen, casting its golden glow on the forest that surrounded their villa. A racket of meows and barking sounded from the barn. Fabrizio whinnied.

"I'm coming. I'm coming!" Serafina said, joining Pamina outside.

Soon it would get too cold for all the outdoor cats and Gio, the little dog that had joined their gang, to stay in the barn and they'd have to move inside the villa. Would the enchanted villa like that?

"Are you going to tell them about your magic?" Serafina asked, matching Pamina's steps.

Her question snapped Pamina to attention. She frowned. "No. Not unless they ask me. I won't lie about it though."

Her sister snorted. "No one ever asks you about your magic. They don't want to know. Not really. Because then they'd have to admit what hypocrites they are. Wrinkling their noses at Liliana's magic but eagerly devouring yours."

Pamina turned to her sister. "Not everyone is against magic, Fina."

Serafina shrugged. "Depends on what kind of magic."

They fell quiet, leaves crunching beneath their boots as they walked. All around the yard, Fiorella's plants and flowers grew wild. Even in the midst of autumn, their sister's magic held firm, keeping everything within the fence green and vibrant. Thankfully, they didn't get many callers so no one was around to see it.

"Is there something on your mind, Fina? You've seemed... unhappy lately," Pamina asked gently.

Her sister's dark eyes snapped to her. "I could say the same about you."

With that, she veered off toward the barn, throwing Pamina a curt wave goodbye. Pamina glanced at the wooden gate before her and debated whether she should take the time to press her sister or not.

She shook off the question and continued to the gate. They could continue the conversation later. She didn't want to show up late on her first day. Signor Bartoli didn't seem the type to be very forgiving of tardiness.

The image of the tall, muscular, brooding half-goblin filled her mind. He didn't look much older than Dante, but there had been no mention of a spouse or fiancé.

Aside from the same strong jawline, Pamina could see very

little of Signor Covelli in him. The memory of Signor Bartoli's dark eyes searing into her made her stomach clench. She hadn't seen him crack as so much as a smile when they'd met. Hopefully, he wouldn't be in a sour mood that day.

His biting words replayed as she closed the gate behind her. He'd made it clear that he had chosen purposefully not to come to his father's funeral. It was obvious he still held resentment for his father leaving them. She'd felt the same hurt at her own father's abandonment, but whether he deserved it or not, she'd chosen to forgive him. Hating him forever would have only made her bitter.

It was hard to believe Signor Covelli had children and a wife before he'd come to Zamerra. Why had he left them? Why had he never mentioned them?

She dismissed the thoughts and hurried down the dirt path. The crisp, mountain air filled her lungs as she passed the Rossis' villa. Alessia and Massimo's villa was in the opposite direction and there had been talk about Liliana and Dante building a home of their own further up the mountain after their wedding.

Fiorella's words rang in Pamina's ears. *Everyone is leaving.*

It wasn't completely true, but Pamina understood how her little sister felt. It mirrored her own feelings. That changes were happening all around her and yet she was left behind.

Pushing the thought away, she continued forward, her breath puffing out in little clouds as she went.

Excitement filled her at the prospect of baking. She'd forgotten her recipe book, but she knew it all by heart. The first thing she'd make, if they had all the ingredients, would be a pie. Pies were great for healing broken hearts. She pulled out a croissant and took a bite, running through different recipes in her head.

Zamerra was quiet as Pamina made her way to the bakery. Only a few people milled about, bundled against the cold, and hurrying to their destinations. Smoke billowed from the chimneys, filling the cloudless sky.

Some of the shops were already decorated for the Harvest Festival. Bright red and orange garlands of leaves were strung from building to building. The festival was one of the busiest times for her family where they made most of the money needed to get through the winter. However, with Alessia and Liliana's newfound wealth, they already had enough. More than enough.

Pamina made it to the bakery and stopped outside the door. The curtains were still drawn closed. She knocked, straining to hear anything on the other side.

Had they arrived yet?

She glanced next door at the Apothecary, wondering if Liliana and Dante were already up and getting ready. Maybe she could stay with them until the bakery opened.

Footsteps sounded behind her, making her turn. It was Signor Bartoli. His silky-looking, black hair was cut short, revealing large, pointed ears.

He looked dashing in his long, brown coat and cream-colored scarf. Pamina couldn't help but notice his broad chest and large arms, the cotton material looking strained as he moved.

Pamina's gaze snapped to his face, heat spreading up her neck at being caught staring at him.

Surprise flashed in his brown eyes. He blinked and shook his head, a frown growing on his face. Pamina glanced around the empty street behind him.

Where was his sister? Would it just be the two of them in the shop?

Chapter 6

The Baking Witch

Lorenzo

Lorenzo stopped short outside the bakery. Pamina had already arrived. How long had she been waiting for them? Irritation filled him at his sister's tardiness. She'd been the one to insist on starting first thing in the morning and then, in typical Giulia fashion, she wasn't ready on time.

Pamina stared up at him, her round cheeks rosy from the cold. A nervous look crossed her features, making him frown. Was it being alone with a strange man that upset her or was it his goblin blood?

While he found her attractive maybe she was equally repulsed by him. Damn Giulia for putting them in this situation. She better be arriving soon.

"Good morning, Signorina. I hope you haven't had to wait in the cold for too long. I'm afraid my sister is running late this morning. She should be along shortly," he said, hoping his words would put her at ease.

Relief flashed on Pamina's face before she broke into a smile. "Oh, I only just arrived, Signor. I don't mind waiting for your sister."

A scoff escaped Lorenzo. "We could be waiting all day. Excuse me, Signorina."

He pulled out the brass key and waited for Pamina to step aside. The smell of fresh caffé and fire drifted from her as she moved out of his path. There was also a subtle smell of her soap, a fresh and clean scent that filled his lungs. Did he detect a faint trace of honey as well?

Pushing the intrusive thought away, Lorenzo walked up to the door and unlocked it. He opened it and waved Pamina in first. She hesitated at the threshold, tugging at the hem of her coat.

Lorenzo watched the war of emotions on her face, curious to see what she did. She was a nervous thing. All doe-eyed and flushed cheeks. Hardly much older than his sister. Did she have a fiancé? The thought startled him. It was none of his concern.

His gaze dipped down, heat pooling inside him. Though he considered himself a gentleman, he couldn't help but notice her luscious curves. The way her cream-colored coat hugged her body...

Lorenzo looked away and coughed, clearing his mind. He was beginning to suspect his sister had somehow picked up on his attraction to Pamina and had purposefully woken later, leaving them alone.

"Thank you," Pamina finally answered, walking past him and into the shop.

He followed her in, closing the door behind them. Darkness enveloped them inside the bakery. Without a fire lit, the shop was freezing. Lorenzo pushed back the red curtains, letting the sunlight stream in from the giant front window.

Everything was quiet. The whole town was quiet compared to the city. It was unnerving, to say the least.

"Should I start with the espresso?" Pamina's question brought Lorenzo's head around.

He glared at the fancy machine. How much had the scoundrel spent on that contraption? Though he'd sent money to their mother when he could, it hadn't been enough. It was their mother who had worked tooth and nail just to scrape up enough money to send both Lorenzo and Giulia to a proper school.

"Or I could start the oven. It's been a while since I've used the gas oven, but I think I can remember how to do it. Signor?" Pamina's gentle voice pulled Lorenzo from his dark memories.

He met her gaze. The sunlight shone on her through the large storefront, highlighting her light brown eyes and flawless tan skin. She was beautiful.

A look of uncertainty crossed her features. Was she frightened of him? It wouldn't be the first time he was judged by appearance alone. Lorenzo glanced out the window, wishing Giulia would hurry up.

The last thing he wanted to do was touch any of the equipment his *father* had left. This was all Giulia's scheme, and she wasn't even there to see it through.

Lorenzo's head ached. He rubbed his forehead and took a deep breath.

"I'm sorry, Signor. I know this must be hard for you. Your father—"

"I don't want to talk about him," he snapped, turning back to face her. "Please."

Her eyes widened. "Oh. Forgive me. I didn't... I didn't mean to offend you."

Guilt filled him at her startled look. Where was Giulia? She was much better equipped for this. His head throbbed and his body tensed up. Though it was freezing in the bakery, Lorenzo felt a wave of heat spreading through him.

His chest constricted, making it hard to breathe. *Fantastic.*

He was about to have a panic attack in front of their new employee.

He clenched his eyes shut and tried to count and steady his breathing.

"Here, eat this. Please," Pamina urged, placing something in his hand.

Lorenzo looked down to find a squished croissant. He gave Pamina a questioning look and held up the pastry for inspection.

Pamina blushed prettily but didn't offer any more explanation. It wasn't the most appetizing looking thing, but he didn't want to hurt her feelings. At least not right away. If this was an example of the woman's *promising* skill, Giulia's plan for the bakery was in trouble.

"Er... thank you?" he said, unable to hide his confusion.

Pamina's face reddened further as he took a hesitant bite. It was cold, but perfectly flaky and soft. Buttery and sweet.

Lorenzo looked at her in surprise. "This is delicious."

She smiled, the sight twisting something inside him. Funny enough, his headache disappeared and his breathing returned to normal. A calmness filled him.

Magic.

He glanced at the croissant and back to Pamina. "What did you put in here?" His question came out harsher than he meant it to.

Pamina flinched, her smile fading. "Well, it's just your usual croissant. With—"

"No. This is not your *usual* croissant. Do you think I'm a fool?"

Her face fell. "No. Of course not, Signor."

"You may have been able to fool Signor Covelli, but I know magic when I see it. Or in this case, taste it."

The distressed look on her face made him instantly regret

his words. He hadn't meant to upset her. He could see now she had only been trying to help him, not trick him.

Before he could apologize, the door swung open, and in marched Giulia. Her smile faltered as she took in Pamina's worried face.

Her gaze snapped to Lorenzo. "Oh, what have you said now, Lor?"

He waved his hands in an appeasement, croissant still in his grasp. Giulia's eyes narrowed on it before turning to Pamina with an embarrassed smile.

"Whatever he said, please forgive him. His manners are lacking, but I assure you, he means no offense. Brother?" She shot him daggers with her eyes.

Lorenzo turned to Pamina and nodded. "My apologies, Signorina. I spoke too harshly. I'm afraid I misjudged you. Where I'm from, those who practice magic... aren't always the most honest folk."

Giulia's eyes widened at this. She shut the front door with a loud 'bang' and strode forward. "Magic? Are you a witch?"

Pamina shrank away from her. Her wary expression stirred something inside Lorenzo. He hardly knew the woman, but he couldn't help but feel the need to protect her and rush to her defense.

"Giulia, did you instruct the driver to unhitch the horse and bring him to the stables?" Lorenzo asked, drawing his sister's attention.

She frowned at him. "No. I told him he could just drop me off and return to the inn."

Lorenzo sighed. "And what if we need to shop around for more supplies? It would have been better to have use of the cart."

Giulia shrugged, turning her attention back to Pamina.

Once his sister's interest was piqued, she was unrelenting. Like a dog with a bone.

"Signora Bianchi told us about your mother and sister, but she didn't mention you were a witch too," his sister pressed.

Seeming to have found her courage, Pamina nodded and spread her arms out in a placating gesture. "Many of the townsfolk aren't very trusting of magic. It was never my intention to deceive you or... Signor Covelli."

"So, you do have magic? My best friend is a witch, but she doesn't have much magic."

Pamina's eyes darted to Lorenzo. "Yes. I'm... I'm a baking witch."

Giulia clapped her hands together. "Oh, that's wonderful! Isn't that wonderful, Lor?"

"Yes. Wonderful," Lorenzo muttered, feeling another headache coming on.

He glanced at the croissant now crushed in his hand. With this new revelation, Giulia would only be all the more eager to continue with this ridiculous charade. Lorenzo was beginning to worry they would be stuck in Zamerra for far longer than he had planned on.

Pamina's questioning look caught his eye. Had she caught his sarcastic tone?

A baking witch. Of all things. How could the old man have missed that? Surely if he'd known of Pamina's talents, he would have hired her instead of Signora Bianchi. Or perhaps he had known and that was the reason he hadn't hired her on.

Dismissing the questions, Lorenzo stuffed the rest of the pastry into his mouth and savored it.

"Well, I'm going to start a fire to warm this place. I'll leave you two to get started on... the baking lessons?"

Giulia waved a hand in his direction, her focus still on

Pamina. "Yes, alright. You should find the instructions for the espresso machine too."

Lorenzo fought the urge to roll his eyes. As much as he didn't want to mess with the gadget, a hot cup of espresso sounded perfect.

Turning away from them, he headed for the little chiminea, trying to keep a positive outlook. Giulia's excited chatter echoed through the bakery. If this crazy endeavor made his sister happy and helped her forget about *Riccardo* then he would play along for the time being. He owed her that much.

Perhaps with Pamina's help, they could turn over a nice profit. At least get something out of their inheritance. Then they could sell it and be on their way. Far away from Zamerra and the distractingly beautiful baking witch.

Wishing he had another croissant, Lorenzo sighed and opened the chiminea door to inspect it. There was nothing but ashes left. He frowned. Where would he find more wood? He hadn't seen a wood stack outside.

Feeling eyes on him, he turned around to see Giulia and Pamina staring at him.

His sister's eyebrow arched. "Everything alright, Lor?"

He bit back his annoyance at their attention and nodded. "Of course. I'll be back."

Before they could ask him any more questions, he hurried out the front door to search for some wood. A cold gust of wind blew past him, biting through his coat. He looked up and down the empty street. Lorenzo didn't know if he was still feeling the effects of Pamina's magical pastry, or if it was the quietness of the town, but there was a peacefulness there he hadn't found in the city.

He looked up at the cloudless, blue sky and sighed. They'd left what few servants they'd had back in the city and as kind as the count's offer was, Lorenzo couldn't very well ask *him* where he could purchase more wood. Why hadn't the old man kept more kindling on hand?

Irresponsible and stupid.

"Signor Bartoli! Good morning," a cheery voice greeted from next door.

Lorenzo turned and nodded politely at his neighbor. Signor Lazzaro stepped out of the apothecary to join him, a wooden crate in his hands. He was wrapped in a ridiculous puffy white coat and cap that contrasted with his dark skin and black curls.

Lorenzo bit back a groan. He'd only had one cup of caffé so far and wasn't in the mood for pleasantries.

Oblivious to his irritation, Signor Lazzaro flashed him a friendly smile. "I saw Pamina has arrived. You'll be in very good hands with her. She's an excellent baker."

Mirth shone in his dark eyes, making Lorenzo's suspicions rise. Had his fiancée, Pamina's sister, put him up to this? Just what were they playing at? Surely, they couldn't be interested in matching the poor girl to the likes of him. With her beauty, she could have any suitor she'd like.

Realizing the man was still watching him and waiting for a response, Lorenzo cleared his throat. "Yes. Well, I would think magic as a secret ingredient would make anything taste good," he answered wryly.

The man's eyebrows shot up. "So, she told you then? About her... skills?"

Lorenzo frowned. "Not directly, but she admitted to it. I'm from Arastula and I know magic when I see it."

A wistful look crossed Signor Lazzaro's face. "Yes, well, all the same, we don't wish to draw too much attention to it. Even with Massimo as count, the people here... are wary of magic."

"You seem to get enough business in your *apothecary*," Lorenzo said, glancing at the shop.

The warlock followed his gaze and shrugged. "Put a pretty

label on it and people can feign ignorance. For all its faults though, Zamerra is actually quite lovely."

Lorenzo sniffed. "I would find it lovelier if it weren't so cold."

"Ahh. Actually, that's what I was sent out here to do. Gather the wood. There's a storeroom of kindling for the shops. We all take turns chopping and replenishing it. Would you like me to show you?"

Lorenzo's eyebrow arched at his words. A communal wood storage? That was definitely something he'd never seen in the city.

"If it's no inconvenience..."

The man grinned. "Of course not. We are neighbors after all."

With that, he turned and led Lorenzo past the storefront and around the corner to the back. Once they had filled the crate with enough firewood for the both of them, they returned to the bakery.

Giulia and Pamina looked up as they entered. They'd removed their coats and were behind the counter, preparing the oven.

Lorenzo inhaled sharply at the sight before him. Pamina wore a long-sleeved dark brown dress and cream-colored apron that hugged her body. Her brown curls were wrapped up and her cheeks were flushed. Her eyes met his.

Tearing his gaze away, he walked over to the chiminea and started filling it with the kindling. Busy with the task, he tuned out their chatter. Signor Lazzaro tipped his hat toward him in farewell before leaving with the rest of the wood.

Lorenzo struck the fire stones together and watched as the kindling sparked. It felt as if a fire had been ignited inside of him as well. He sighed. Ignoring the beautiful witch was going to be much harder than he thought.

Chapter 7

The Grumpy Goblin
Pamina

The next day, Pamina awoke early, excitement filling her at the prospect of returning to the bakery. This time she would be sure to bring her recipe book. Though a little unskilled, she'd found Giulia to be an apt student and there was a brightness about her that was infectious. She could not, however, say the same about her brother.

Aside from the harsh words he'd spoken to her, he'd made no attempt to talk to her. Instead, he'd spent nearly the whole day in the back room attending to the books. Still, Pamina couldn't help but notice him when he was nearby. It wasn't just his large figure that proved intimidating, but he had a presence about him that drew her attention.

His dark eyes flashed in her mind. Several times, she'd caught him looking at her, but unlike the frank stares or sometimes critical looks she was used to, she couldn't interpret his thoughts.

"Do you have to go back to the bakery today?" Fiorella's question startled her from her doorway.

Pamina sat up in bed and motioned her sister closer.

Fiorella's stockinged feet thumped loudly against the wood as she hurried to Pamina's side. Once they were both snug under the warm quilt, backs against the headboard, Pamina rested her head against Fiorella's.

"Yes. I'm going to be very busy for the next few weeks, I'm afraid. There is much to do before they can reopen the bakery."

Fiorella sighed. "When can I come and visit? Do you think they'd let me help too?"

The hopefulness in her sister's voice made Pamina wince. She hated that Fiorella was feeling left out, but couldn't see Signor Bartoli allowing another witch into the shop. Despite Giulia's insistence that her brother approved of her magic, Pamina suspected that was not the case.

"I can ask about you visiting, Ella, but I think it would be best if you stayed here to help Mama and Serafina. With the vegetables for the harvest."

Fiorella frowned. "It won't be the same."

"What? The festival? Why not? We'll all be there, Ella. Just like always."

Her sister shook her head. "It's not. It's not like always, Pamina. Alessia and Liliana will be too busy to help us with the vegetables, and now you'll be busy with the bakery."

"You'll still have Serafina," Pamina tried to soothe her.

Fiorella huffed. "She's no fun anymore. All she can talk about is Angelo and Valentina. She said Valentina is a brainless twit so she'd make a perfect match for Angelo."

Her sister's words made her frown. Perhaps that was why Serafina had been so sour lately. She made a note to talk to her about it when she got home.

"I'm sorry, Ella. I'll talk to the others and see what we can do. Maybe it's time we have a girls' day. Would you like that?"

Fiorella's face brightened. "Oh, yes!"

Her smile faltered, "but I don't want to hurt Dante or

Massimo's feelings. I love them both dearly, you know. It's just..."

"Of course, you do. They know that. I'm sure they'll be more than fine with us having a sisters' day. Now, why don't you think about what you'd like to do and we can make some plans when I get back. Alright?"

Fiorella turned to hug her tightly. "Thank you."

The wobbliness in her sister's voice made Pamina's heart twist. Guilt filled her. With Alessia and Liliana out of the villa, it was up to her to make sure her sisters were happy. How selfish of her to only think of herself.

Looking much happier, Fiorella threw off the covers and swung her feet to the floor.

"I'm going to wake up Fina and tell her!" she exclaimed, disappearing down the hall before Pamina could warn her against it. Serafina was a bear in the morning. Even worse than little Bruno.

After dressing and readying herself, Pamina went down to make a quick breakfast for Mama and the girls. Before they came down, she finished off her giant mug of caffé and said goodbye to the villa.

* * *

"Good morning!" Signorina Bartoli greeted Pamina at the entrance of the bakery.

"Good morning, Signorina." Pamina returned her greeting with a smile.

"Please, just call me Giulia," the young half-goblin said, opening the door wider to let Pamina through.

Pamina stepped inside, shaking off the cold. A fire blazed from the stone chiminea in the corner, filling the bakery with warmth. The smoky smell of burnt bread struck Pamina's nose.

Giulia gave her a sheepish look. "I'm afraid I left the croissants in too long."

Pamina smiled gently. "Oh, that's alright. We can make more."

She glanced around at the empty shop, a wave of sorrow filling her. Though she'd only come occasionally to help Signor Covelli, she had many fond memories of him teaching her when she was younger.

It was hard for her to reconcile the image of the kind older man with the same man who had left his wife and children. Why had he left them?

"Here, let me take that," Giulia chirped, reaching a hand toward the basket she carried.

Pamina nodded in thanks as she handed it to her and started removing her coat. She hung it up on the rack beside Giulia's, noticing that her brother's coat was missing. Had he decided to stay at the inn to do his paperwork?

Disappointment filled her at the thought.

"Oh, what is this?" Giulia's question brought her head around.

She had pulled out the giant jar of pumpkin puree Pamina had brought and was eyeing it with excitement.

"It's for the pumpkin pie. It came from a pumpkin from our garden," Pamina said.

Giulia's eyes widened. "You think I'm ready to learn how to make a pie? Yesterday didn't go so well."

Pamina gave her a kind smile. "It was your first day. I'll help you with each step. It won't be too hard."

A look of uncertainty flashed across Giulia's face, but she shrugged and led Pamina to the long marble counter. The dress the young woman wore today, while still fancier than anything Pamina owned, wasn't as poofy as the one she had yesterday.

That would make it much easier to get around in the small kitchen.

After washing and drying their hands, Pamina took charge pulling all the items out of the basket and laying them out on the counter.

Giulia smiled. "I've never made a pumpkin pie before. This will be fun. I can't wait to show my brother!"

The image of Giulia's brother sprang into Pamina's mind. His dark, stormy eyes and strong jawline. His mere presence made her feel strange. On edge. Mostly because she wasn't sure how to read his mood.

Pushing the image away, Pamina turned to gather the rest of the supplies they would need. A bowl and whisk for mixing. A pie tin. Measuring cups.

"Here is a list of the ingredients," Pamina said, opening her giant recipe book to the correct page. She tapped a finger on the handwritten list. Giulia moved closer to take a look.

"We have all this, I believe. All except the eggs. I'll send Lor out for that when he gets here."

Pamina's heart skipped at the mention of the handsome man. She shook her head, trying to clear her thoughts.

Misreading her reaction, Giulia snorted. "It's fine. Trust me. He'll be happy for an excuse to not be here."

Her words made Pamina frown. Was it her presence that bothered him so?

Before Giulia could see her hurt, Pamina turned away and headed for the spice cabinet. Keeping herself busy helped her manage her emotions. She opened the wooden cabinet and ran a hand along the labeled tins. A smile tugged at her lips.

If only they had such a variety at home for her own personal use. Images of the things she'd make flitted through her mind. The sound of the front door opening startled her out of her thoughts.

"Oh, Lor. There you are. Will you go buy some eggs from the general store?" Giulia turned to her. "How many do you think we'll need?"

Pamina didn't hear her question. Her eyes met Lorenzo's, his gaze dark and unreadable. There was a light dusting of white on his clothes and in his dark hair.

Giulia squealed. "Is it snowing?"

Eggs forgotten, she hurried away from the counter to go look out the window. Pamina followed, just as excited. Giulia's enthusiasm was contagious.

Signor Bartoli stepped out of their path, an irritated look on his face. "Yes. And I forgot my hat."

Pamina's gaze slid from the window to him. She couldn't help but smile at the grumpy goblin. He brushed the snow from his hair with an aggravated sigh. Pamina had the strange urge to run her fingers through his silky-looking hair and help him.

His eyes locked with hers. Something unreadable passed across his face. Heat flooded her, and suddenly the bakery felt too warm.

"Eggs then?" he asked, turning his attention back to his sister.

She glanced at him. "I can get them. I didn't forget *my* hat."

He frowned at her. "Shouldn't you stay here and help Signorina Silveri?"

Giulia turned back to the window and sighed. "I suppose so. Though it seems a shame to miss the first snow of the season."

Her brother snorted. "I'd hardly call it the first snow. It's barely a dusting."

Seeming to have forgotten her, the two siblings exchanged silent, stubborn looks. His back to her now, Pamina waited, unsure of what to do. She could smell the fresh air on his coat. There was also a subtle smell of soap and something *woodsy*.

He turned to her abruptly, making her eyes snap to his and her face flush.

"Is there anything else you need, Signorina?"

His deep voice sent a shiver of awareness through her. Unable to trust herself to talk, Pamina shook her head at his question.

"What about your head? You'll catch a cold, Lor," Giulia said in a motherly tone.

Her brother looked from her to Pamina. "Well then, it's a good thing we know a witch with healing powers."

"Oh, well, my spells are only temporary. But my sister can perform longer-lasting healing spells," Pamina said.

"Yes, and she probably charges an arm and a leg for it," he said with a scoff.

"Lorenzo!" Giulia scolded him.

She shot Pamina an apologetic look before grabbing hold of her brother's arm and leading him toward the back room.

Pamina bit back a smile as she watched the smaller woman practically drag her giant of a brother away.

Though his words were offensive, Pamina couldn't help but compare his sharp tongue to that of her sister. Truth be told, if Liliana had heard him, she'd probably have something just as smarting to say in return. Dante would laugh.

Giulia and Lorenzo reappeared, a chastised look on the latter's face. After a tight-lipped apology to her, Lorenzo left the bakery in a hurry.

"You'll have to forgive him. I don't mean to make excuses for his behavior, but he's had a rough time of it late... well... always. First, with our father leaving and well growing up half-goblin wasn't easy. He had it worse than I did. Then with his fiancée breaking off their engagement, and then losing our mother..."

Giulia's words echoed in her mind. Fiancée? Lorenzo had been engaged?

Dismissing the questions, Pamina turned to her. "I'm sorry to hear about your mother's passing. I can't imagine how difficult it must be to lose both parents," she said.

Giulia gave her a sad smile. "It is, but we have each other. Part of me is thankful that my own engagement fell through. If it hadn't... I would hate for my brother to be all alone."

"You were engaged?" Pamina couldn't hide the surprise in her voice.

"Yes. To a very wealthy man in the city."

"What happened?"

Giulia scoffed and waved a hand down her body. "This happened."

Seeing Pamina's confusion, she continued. "His family didn't approve of my *heritage*, and he was too much of a coward to go against them."

Pamina frowned. "Oh, Giulia, I'm so sorry. He must have been a fool to let you go over something so trivial as that."

Giulia shrugged and gave her a tight smile that didn't reach her eyes.

What else could Pamina say? It was unimaginable that someone could overlook all of Giulia's good qualities simply because her mother had been a goblin. Though, even in Zamerra, people were quick to judge others.

"So, should we start on the pie or do we need to wait for my brother?" Giulia's question snapped her back to the present.

"We'll need the eggs, but we can start on something else, if you'd like? Do you want to try the croissants again? Or we can try to figure out the espresso machine."

Giulia walked behind the counter and Pamina followed. She watched as Giulia flipped through her cookbook, the sound filling the silence. Giulia's mouth pursed as she skimmed the pages.

After deciding on cinnamon rolls, Pamina instructed Giulia on each step. Though her hands were busy, her mind kept straying back to Giulia's words.

Lorenzo had been engaged. Curiosity filled her. Who had he been promised to and what happened? Perhaps that was what made him so surly. Sometimes the most wounded hearts were the prickliest.

She glanced at the abandoned ingredients for the pumpkin pie. Now more than ever she believed he needed it. Pies were perfect for broken hearts. Would he accept it from her, though? Pamina doubted he would appreciate his sister divulging his story to her.

Giulia sighed, the noise bringing Pamina out of her thoughts.

"I need a break. Do you want to walk over with me next door to your sister's shop?"

Pamina glanced at the oven. "I should wait here to keep an eye on the rolls. If that's alright with you?"

"Of course. How silly of me."

She glanced out the front window with a wistful look.

"But you don't have to stay, Giulia. I'll be here. You should get some fresh air."

"Are you sure you don't mind? You're okay with staying here?" Giulia asked.

Pamina nodded. "Of course. I'm perfectly happy with staying in the kitchen."

"Thank you! You are amazing, Pamina," the young woman squealed as she hurried to grab her coat and hat.

Pamina watched her leave and turned back to the oven. She meant what she'd said. Though she loved her little kitchen in their villa, she'd found herself quite content in the bakery kitchen. The gas oven was almost as good as magic.

A few minutes later, the rolls were ready. Pamina opened the oven and bent down with cloths on her hands to pull them out. A sharp intake of breath sounded behind her, making her jump.

She quickly set the tray atop the stove and turned around.

Lorenzo was back and he didn't look happy.

Chapter 8

The Invitation

Lorenzo

The image of Pamina's lovely backside was seared into Lorenzo's mind. Thankfully, he'd regained his senses enough to not drop the eggs he'd been requested to bring.

"Oh, Signor. You startled me," Pamina said with a short laugh.

Lorenzo blinked and glanced around. "Where is Giulia?"

Pamina's smile faded. "She needed some fresh air. She should be back any moment."

That was just like Giulia to get bored and wander off.

He scowled. "You shouldn't have let her leave and shirk her duties."

Pamina's eyebrow arched at his tone.

He cleared his throat and attempted to soften his words. "Forgive me, Signorina, I didn't mean to speak so harshly."

How many more times would he have to apologize to the poor woman?

She gave him a wry smile. "Yes, well you seem to have a habit of that, Signor."

Her quip surprised him. Maybe she wasn't as nervous and timid as he'd believed. Or maybe she was growing more comfortable around him. That would simply not do.

"Well, I mean no disrespect. I'll do my best to not speak so... severely. I've brought the eggs you needed," Lorenzo said, walking over to her with the brown bag holding the carton of eggs.

The smell of the cinnamon rolls wafted through the shop, making his mouth water. Did she bake them with magic like she had the croissants? Could she bake at all without using her power?

"Thank you!" she exclaimed, taking the bag from him, and interrupting his thoughts.

Her fingers brushed his. The touch was soft and brief, but the effect it left was powerful. Lorenzo felt as if his hand had caught fire. Could she feel it too?

She was so close. The warmth from her body enveloped him and that subtle honey smell of her soap invaded his senses. What would it feel like to reach out and wrap his arms around her? Hold her tight and feel those luscious curves...

He should move away. Go and hunt down his irresponsible sister. A walk in the icy cold would be just what he needed to cool himself.

Instead, he stepped closer and leaned over her to peer at the open cookbook on the counter. "What are you making now?" he heard himself ask, his voice dipping deeper.

Pamina shuddered. It was slight but obvious.

Afraid he'd frightened her, he stepped away, giving them both space.

Pamina turned to him, eyes pinning his boldly. "Pie. A pumpkin pie."

Lorenzo blinked, his brain taking a while to catch up with

her. What was he doing? Oh, he'd asked her what she was making. *Right.*

She didn't say anything else, but the burning look of desire in her gaze was unmistakable. Her chest was rising slowly, her cheeks flushed, and her lips slightly parted. Welcoming.

He bit back a groan. Just a few steps forward and their lips would meet. Did she taste as sweet as she smelled?

Before he could act on his impulses, the front door swung open, making them both jump.

Giulia's eyes darted between them, a sly smile growing on her face.

"Why, Lor, I didn't know you were interested in taking baking lessons too," she said with an innocent look.

Lorenzo scowled in return and straightened his coat. "And where have you been?"

Giulia grinned. "Next door. Oh, and guess what, brother? We've been invited to dinner! Isn't that marvelous?"

"A dinner? With whom? We don't know anyone here."

"Signor Rossi invited us. He lives up the mountain with his husband."

"Oh, the Rossis are our neighbors! They're wonderful. You'll have a great time," Pamina said with a sweet smile.

Giulia nodded. "As will you. They invited your sister and her fiancé. And all your family too."

Lorenzo shot a dark look at his sister, who dutifully ignored it. Dinner with Pamina and her family? Was his sister trying to vex him?

"Giulia, can I have a word with you please?"

"Oh, we should bring the pie! It will be the first sample of our bakery," she rambled on, ignoring him.

"Giulia."

"And I'll have to go back to the inn and change. I can't wear

68

this for a dinner party! Lor, you should change too. Don't forget your hat."

Lorenzo walked toward her, his patience growing thin. "Giulia, please."

He motioned for her to step outside with him. With a loud huff, she followed him, casting Pamina an apologetic look.

Icy air struck them as they stepped out under the awning.

"Why would you accept an invitation without my consent?" Lorenzo asked, trying to remain cool-headed.

Giulia's face hardened. "Because if I had asked you, you would have said no."

"Of course, I would have said no. *You* should have said no. The last thing I want to do is have dinner with a bunch of strangers."

She folded her arms across her chest. "They knew our father, Lor. We—"

A harsh laugh escaped him. "That makes me want to go even less. Giulia, the last thing we should be doing is putting down roots here. Here of all places. Now, I've allowed you to move forward with this ridiculous bakery idea, but this—"

"You've *allowed* me?" Giulia's eyes narrowed. "Allowed me?" she repeated, though he knew it wasn't because she'd misheard him.

"You know what I mean," he said with a sigh. He didn't want to fight with her.

"I didn't ask you to stay, Lor. You made that choice." Her tone was steely.

"Well, of course, I did. I couldn't leave you here by yourself."

Giulia scoffed. "I'm not a child, Lor. I can do this with or without you."

Her words cut through him like a knife. It was true, she'd

always been independent, but now more so than ever. He needed her more than she needed him.

Seeing his reaction, her face softened. "But I'd much rather we did this together. Like we do everything, but if you are truly unhappy here, I won't ask you to stay. You know I couldn't do that to you."

A knowing look crossed her face. "Though you didn't look all that unhappy just now in the bakery with Pamina."

Lorenzo shot her a flat look. *Pamina.* Since when was his sister on a first-name basis with the young witch? It was just like Giulia to make friends and collect dinner invitations as if it were the easiest thing in the world.

He sighed and rubbed his forehead. "I'm here for you, Giulia. Only you. For as long as you need me to be here."

She hugged him. "What if I never want to leave? What if I want to make a home here?"

Lorenzo sucked in a breath. That was one of his fears. As much as he loved his sister and wanted to help her, he couldn't see himself staying in Zamerra indefinitely. This place held nothing for him. Not even a certain baking witch could change that.

"Should it come to that, we'll... figure it out," he finally said, wrapping his arms around his sister.

She sighed into his chest and looked up at him with a mischievous look. "So, what were you two doing while I was next door?"

Lorenzo frowned and released her. "What do you mean? I was simply observing her work."

Giulia snorted. "Her work, huh? Looked more like you were observing *her.*"

"Giulia!" he admonished her, darting a look around the empty street. His sister wasn't exactly discreet.

Giulia smiled smugly. "Aha! I knew it. You like her, don't you?"

Heat spread up his neck. "Kindly lower your voice, please. And stop at once with this absurd notion. She's an attractive woman, but I have no interest in pursuing anything with her or any other woman in this town for that matter."

A pitying look crossed his sister's face. "Oh, Lor. Don't you think it's been long enough since Niccola?"

His chest tightened at the mention of his ex-fiancé. He'd been in love with her, but she had fallen in love with another man. The memory of it was still fresh, but the pain had dulled.

Deep down, Lorenzo knew it was for the better. They'd wanted different things. It wouldn't have worked in the end anyway. Or at least that's what he told himself.

"Lor?" Giulia asked, worry swimming in her brown eyes.

He shook off the memories. "I'll agree to this dinner on one account, Giulia. You stop trying to play matchmaker for me. Can you do that?"

His sister looked as if she was going to argue, but stopped herself. She nodded. "Yes. Fine. I'll stay out of it."

With that, she turned and went inside the bakery. Lorenzo followed, sucking in a lungful of cold air before entering. He needed to steel himself against the effects of Pamina Silveri.

The sweet smell of the cinnamon rolls filled the shop. Warmth from the oven and the chiminea spread through him. He stamped his boots on the little rug and hung his coat beside his sister's and Pamina's.

Giulia was already back behind the counter, gushing over the pastries.

"Lor, come try one! Don't they look so beautiful?" She waved him over.

He didn't trust himself not to stare at Pamina, so he didn't look her way. Instead, he kept his eyes focused on his sister as he joined them.

"This would go so well with some espresso," Giulia said, giving him a pointed look.

Lorenzo glanced at the shiny machine in the corner. He'd found the instructions but wasn't sure he could bring himself to mess around with the thing. Every time he saw it, he pictured the old man using it or cleaning it. Taking more care with that then he had his own children.

"Oh, I can try to get it going, if you like?" Pamina's soft voice pulled him from his thoughts.

Giulia clapped her hands. "That would be lovely! I've been craving a nice cup of espresso since we've arrived."

"They have espresso at the inn," Lorenzo said flatly.

She scowled at him. "It's not the same. This is a very sophisticated machine, Lor. Probably even better than the one we've had in the city."

He bit back a scoff. "It's just espresso."

His sister's scowl deepened. Lorenzo knew better than to keep needling her, but he'd inherited just as much of a stubborn streak as she had.

Pamina cleared her throat, getting their attention. "I can bring some of my own special brew tomorrow if you like. But for today, I can try and get the machine working."

"Yes, please," Giulia said, giving Lorenzo a look that dared him to argue with Pamina.

He sighed and turned to leave. There was a pile of papers to sort through in the back and though the prospect of leafing through them made his lip curl, he liked the idea of using his father's equipment even less.

Besides, he needed to get away from Pamina and clear his mind. Especially since he was being forced to go and have dinner with her and her family. How would he survive a whole evening in her presence?

"Did my father show you how to work the machine?" Giulia's question rang in his ears as he left them.

Lorenzo fought the urge to correct her. There was that word again. *Father.* Though the man had wed their mother, sired them, sent them money, and came to visit off and on, he wasn't their father. Not in any real sense of the word.

If he had loved their mother, if he had loved them, why hadn't he brought them to Zamerra with him? What would their life have been like if they'd grown up there? Grown up alongside Pamina?

Lorenzo dismissed the questions, pushing the images of the witch out of his mind. It was too late to go back and change the past. All he could do was move forward.

The back room was freezing and bleak. A small window above the sink let in a little sunlight, but not enough to keep warm. Lorenzo sighed and debated if he should start a fire in the hearth or go back up front to get his coat.

Laughter drifted from the shop. He could picture the two women chatting and baking, becoming quick friends. It was good for Giulia. She needed a companion now that she was so far from her city friends. Pamina would be good for her.

Good for you too. A thought struck him.

Lorenzo scoffed. *Too good for me.*

Pamina deserved someone much better than a miserable goblin like him. She probably already had a suitor. Another thought struck him, making his chest tighten.

What if she brought her suitor to dinner that night? Heat crept up his neck and his throat went dry. Why, oh why, had he agreed to go with Giulia? Parties were her thing, not his.

His ears rang. Before he succumbed to a panic attack, he

sank into the wooden chair by the little table and counted his breaths.

A loud 'pop' sounded followed by shrieks. Lorenzo shot to his feet and burst through the door.

"What is it? What's happened?" he asked, looking around.

Giulia pointed to the espresso machine, one hand over her mouth. Pamina stood next to it, espresso splattered all over her chest. A mug lay broken on the ground at their feet.

Pamina's eyes were wide in horror.

"I'm sorry! I don't know what happened. I followed the instructions. I don't understand," she blabbered, looking on the verge of tears.

She bent down to pick up the pieces of ceramic. Seeing, her distress, Lorenzo bent to help. He reached for her hand, stopping her.

Her gaze snapped to his. Could she feel it too? Did her body thrum with the contact as his did?

"Are you alright?" he asked, inspecting her for any injuries.

What if the liquid had burned her? Or the mug cut her?

She gaped at him. "Yes... I think so. Only..." She looked down at the dark liquid staining the front of her blouse.

Lorenzo's gaze dipped to it as well.

Giulia cleared her throat behind him and handed him a wet rag. He took it and offered it to Pamina before helping her to her feet.

She started cleaning herself up, glancing at the mess on the ground. "I can clean this up. And if I've broken the machine, I can repay you, of course. It might take me some time, but I—"

Lorenzo held up a hand to her. "Please, Signorina. It's just a machine. We'll get it fixed. Truth be told, I was thinking of having it replaced, anyway."

Giulia snorted. She bent to finish cleaning up the mug,

ignoring the glare he shot her. Lorenzo thought he heard a muttered 'insufferable' and 'donkey's ass.'

Suddenly the espresso machine spluttered.

Giulia leapt to her feet with a yelp, eyes wide as saucers.

Lorenzo laughed at the sight. Surprise flashed on Pamina's face and Giulia huffed, giving him a playful slap. It felt good to laugh. He couldn't remember the last time he had done it.

His eyes snagged on Pamina. She met his stare, a small smile on her lips. It was a beautiful thing—her smile. Maybe it wasn't just her baking that could heal.

Lorenzo pushed the thought away. Far, far away where it belonged. This was only temporary. He couldn't fall for the beautiful witch.

Chapter 9

The Dinner Date

Pamina

It was nice and toasty by the fire in the Rossis' sitting room. Pamina sat with her younger sisters, her eyes darting across the room. Snippets of conversation floated around her, but she was too distracted to pay any attention to it.

Where were Lorenzo and Giulia? Had they decided not to come? The snow had stopped before it could even coat the ground so there was no danger driving up the mountain. Liliana and Dante were proof of that, having come from town themselves.

So, where were her employers?

Pamina glanced at Salvatore, the question on the tip of her tongue. *No.* She couldn't ask that. It wasn't any of her business and asking would only put Mama on high alert.

Pamina turned to look at her mother. Mama Silveri's dark eyes studied her, a shrewd look on her face. There was little they could hide from her. She was a seer, after all, though she hadn't had a vision in some time.

"A cake would be lovely, no? Pamina?" Alessia's question caught Pamina off guard.

She shifted to face her older sister, sitting across from her, Massimo's arm draped behind her along the couch. Everyone was looking at Pamina now.

"I'm sorry, a cake?" Pamina asked, face growing warm.

Serafina huffed beside her. "I don't want a cake. Shouldn't it be my choice? It is my birthday after all."

Liliana, who had moved to stand by the fire, rolled her eyes. "As if you'd let us forget it."

Serafina shot her a vicious look.

"Well, of course, it's your choice, Fina. I just thought a cake would be nice," Alessia said gently, shaking her head in warning to Liliana.

"How about tiramisu?" Fiorella suggested.

"How about no. You can have tiramisu when it's *your* birthday, Ella," Serafina replied.

"Fina," Pamina and Alessia scolded her in unison.

Pamina glanced at their hosts, heat spreading across her skin. She hadn't had time to make the enchanted cannoli her sister liked nor had she had time to talk to her. Hopefully, Serafina's sour mood wouldn't spoil the dinner.

"I love tiramisu," Angelo, the younger Rossi, piped in with a wide grin.

Serafina turned to him with a scowl. "Nobody asked you, Angelo."

"Serafina!" Pamina exclaimed, shooting an exasperated look to their mother. Why wasn't she intervening?

"Serafina, where are your manners?" Alessia added, frowning.

Liliana snorted. "She must have forgotten them at home along with her gloves."

Face reddening, Serafina sprang up from the couch. Before her sister could further embarrass herself or them, a knock sounded from the front door.

Everyone fell silent.

Salvatore, who'd been watching their exchange with amusement, rose from his seat. "That must be Signorina Bartoli and her brother!"

He excused himself with a quick bow and disappeared out of the room. Pamina's pulse quickened. Suddenly the room felt much too warm. She picked up her glass of water and sipped it, trying to calm herself. What was wrong with her? Was she... nervous?

The memory of Lorenzo's laugh replayed in her mind. It was deep and hearty. Alluring. She shook her head at herself. Could a laugh be alluring?

Giulia's voice sounded from the front, bright and friendly. She didn't hear Lorenzo at all. Surely, she hadn't come without her brother.

"Everyone, please welcome our guests. Signor and Signorina Bartoli," Salvatore announced, leading the newcomers into the sitting room.

Pamina stood along with everyone else, her heart racing. Giulia was dressed in a beautiful golden gown, but it was Lorenzo who stole her breath.

He wore a sleek black evening suit that looked just as silky as his hair. It sheathed his giant frame nicely and complimented his olive-green skin. His dark eyes found hers.

The memory of his nearness in the bakery made her face grow warm. He'd been so close. So close she could smell his distinctly male scent.

Heat washed over her. Male scent? *Santo Cielo.* What was wrong with her?

"Aren't you going to say hello?" Fiorella's confused whisper broke her thoughts.

Horror filled her as she realized everyone was watching her.

She dipped into a polite curtsy, face on fire. "Good evening, Signor. Signorina,"

Giulia waved away her address with a dismissive hand. "Please. Just call me Giulia. That goes for everyone." She grinned.

Her brother shook his head at her impropriety, but said nothing. Pamina watched as the conversation picked back up and questions flew. Lorenzo stood silent amongst it all, his gaze never wavering from her.

"Pamina, he's staring at you," Fiorella said, her words much louder than they needed to be.

She shot her little sister a silencing look.

Out of the corner of her eye, she caught her mother whispering in the corner with Serafina, whose lip curled with defiance.

Oh, no.

Couldn't her sister behave herself for one night? While her mother might find Serafina's antics endearing, she imagined Lorenzo and his sister would not.

Everyone crowded around the siblings, eager to make their acquaintance. Giulia glowed under their attention but Lorenzo looked as if he wanted to be anywhere but there.

Was it crowds he disliked or was it her family? Her stomach churned. They could be a bit much at times...

Fiorella tugged at her dress. "Pamina," she said in a hushed tone.

Pamina turned to her. "What is it?"

"Can you ask them about me helping in the bakery?" her sister pleaded with a hopeful look.

Pamina bit her lip. She had hoped Fiorella would forget about that. Not that she didn't want her sister in the shop with her, but Fiorella's magic was uncontrollable. Anything that came from nature that she touched would be transformed and there was nothing they could do to stop it.

"I can wear my gloves," Fiorella added as if reading her mind.

The gloves she'd been gifted by Dante were enchanted to smother and hold her magic. But if Lorenzo could sense Pamina's magic, he could probably sense Fiorella's too. Even with the gloves. That would not do. Though Pamina trusted him not to give away Fiorella's secret, she worried what his reaction would do to her sister's already fragile self-esteem.

"Pamina?" Fiorella pressed, green eyes narrowing on her.

Pamina sighed. "Ella, we talked about that. Remember? Mama and Serafina need your help with the vegetables for harvest. But you can help me bake any time at home."

Her sister's face fell, making Pamina's insides twist. *Poor Ella.* It wasn't her fault her magic was so volatile. She glanced at Alessia and Liliana. Maybe they would have some ideas as to what to do. Fiorella's magic would only grow stronger as she grew and soon they wouldn't be able to ignore it anymore.

"Dinner is ready, friends," Salvatore's rich voice boomed.

Everyone fell silent and followed him to the dining room. Adriano offered his arm to Pamina and Angelo stepped forward to walk Fiorella. Serafina and Mama were already paired with Salvatore, their host.

It was an old-fashioned custom, but Pamina loved it. If only she'd been paired with Lorenzo. The thought made her blush. Would he have offered her his arm if they'd been side by side? What would it feel like to be escorted by the handsome goblin? It was a silly notion and one she needed to put a stop to immediately.

She caught the back of Lorenzo's head as he walked through the doorway with Giulia on his arm. Trying to push all thoughts of him from her mind, she turned to Adriano.

He gave her a knowing smile that made her face warm. Had he seen her staring at their guest?

"How are things going at the bakery, Signorina?" he asked politely, turning his gaze ahead.

"Well, I believe."

Their heavy footsteps echoed through the hall, conversation blurring together as everyone made their way through.

"Will they be reopening any time soon? And will you stay on when they do?" the giant faun asked, his voice gentle.

His question startled Pamina. Would they ask her to stay? She couldn't help but smile at that possibility, but what about her duties at home? She could do both, couldn't she?

Realizing she hadn't answered, she shook away the thoughts. "I think we'll be open in time for the Harvest Festival. As for staying on... well, they haven't asked me and I haven't thought about it."

Adriano nodded but didn't ask any more questions. When they arrived at the dining room, Pamina's eyes ran along the place settings, hope stirring in her heart.

They'd placed her between Mama and Serafina, at the end across from Angelo and Fiorella. Giulia and Lorenzo were at the opposite end, near the hosts and couples.

Disappointment and embarrassment washed over her. Swallowing her hurt, Pamina forced a smile as Adriano pulled out her chair. The large faun nodded and took his place by his husband.

Mama inclined her head to her. "Everything alright, *amore*?"

"Of course," she replied brightly.

Pamina refused to meet her gaze, afraid her mother would read her emotions. She pasted on a smile and rose her wine glass as Salvatore toasted their honored guests.

Giulia beamed and nodded to them regally while her

brother glanced longingly at the door. The words Giulia had spoken earlier echoed in Pamina's mind.

His fiancée...

His fiancée had broken off their engagement. Why? Was it for the same reason Giulia's beau had broken theirs?

As she stared at Lorenzo, pity filled her. Was his surliness a result of a life full of heartache?

His eyes snapped to hers. One dark eyebrow arched in question. His lips pursed. She'd never seen a man with such sensuous lips.

Tearing her gaze away, Pamina took a sip of the sweet wine, letting it slide down her throat. Warmth flooded her. The whole dining room felt stuffy now. Steam rose from the giant platter of risotto in the middle of the long table. The savory smell of the squash and fresh herbs mixed in filled Pamina's nose.

Pamina scooped a healthy spoonful onto her plate along with the warm bread and roasted potatoes. Since no one paid any attention to her, she quickly threw a contentment spell onto her slice of bread before dipping it into the oil set before her.

The spell rushed through her, making her body relax. It wouldn't last all night, but at least it would last until dessert.

Fiorella and Serafina were unnaturally quiet as they ate, their eyes downcast. Mama had turned her attention to the other side of the table, talking with Alessia and Liliana. That left Pamina to entertain poor Angelo who had been trying, unsuccessfully, to pull Serafina into a conversation all night.

"Will the rest of your family be attending the Harvest Festival?" Pamina asked politely, drawing Angelo's attention.

The young man paused mid-bite and looked at her. "My family will be there, yes."

He forked the risotto into his mouth and chewed slowly before finishing. "But I'm afraid I won't be there this year."

This caught her sister's attention. Serafina's head snapped

up, her dark eyes narrowing at him. "You're not coming to the festival?"

"Why not?" Fiorella asked, abandoning her plate to frown at Angelo.

Angelo sucked in a breath, eyes darting to Serafina. "My uncle offered me an apprenticeship and I've accepted."

"What? Where?" Serafina demanded.

Everyone turned to look at them, but Angelo and Serafina didn't seem to notice the attention they'd drawn.

"He owns a horse ranch in Savoli. It will take nearly two weeks to get there and with the chance of snow coming early, I... I'm leaving next week. "

Fiorella gasped. "But what about Serafina's birthday?"

Angelo's gaze flickered to her. "Oh, I wouldn't miss that. I leave the day after."

He turned his attention back to Serafina. "It's only for two years. I'll be back before you know it."

Pamina felt her sister stiffen beside her. She reached for her hand, but before she could touch her, Serafina pulled away. A war of emotions flashed across her face.

"Congratulations. I'm sure you will do very well," Pamina spoke for her, offering Angelo a smile.

"Yes, we're all very proud of him, but we will miss him dearly," Salvatore said, giving his younger brother an affectionate look.

Angelo was the only one of Salvatore's brothers brave enough to come to his dinners despite his mother's forbidding. She didn't approve of Adriano.

Murmurs of congratulations rippled down the table. Serafina shot to her feet, the sound of her chair scraping the floor loud in the silence.

"Excuse me," she bit out before hurrying out of the room.

Pamina rose too. "I'll go check on her."

Fiorella moved to follow, but Mama stopped her with a shake of her head. As she walked past the others, Pamina noticed the empty chair beside Giulia. Where was Signor Bartoli? When had he left? Had he seen her sister's outburst?

Dismissing the questions, she quickened her pace down the hall. *Poor Serafina.* Angelo's news had been a surprise to all of them, but even more so for her sister. They'd grown up together and while they liked to rile each other with their childish pranks and banter, everyone knew they were smitten.

"Fina?" Pamina called as she paused by the sitting room.

It was empty. Further down the hall, the front door slammed shut. Pamina bit back a groan. As much as she didn't want to go out into the cold, she couldn't just abandon her sister in time of need.

The thought of Serafina huddled somewhere, lost in her grief, urged her forward. After putting on her coat, gloves, and hat, Pamina stepped outside.

She blinked against the darkness. Why hadn't she brought a lamp with her? Cold swirled around her and her breath puffed out as she walked.

"Serafina!" she called.

A whinny sounded from the stables. Light shone from there as well. Pamina turned toward it, leaves crunching under her boots.

"Fina?" She opened the stable doors and stepped inside.

Serafina stood by the horses, her back to Pamina and a lantern in her hand. "I'm fine," she said.

Her voice sounded choked. Very clearly not fine.

"Oh, Fina. I know this must be so hard for you—"

Serafina whipped toward her, eyes blazing. "I said I'm fine."

Pamina sighed. It seemed her sister wasn't ready to talk. Seeing her so upset made Pamina's chest ache. Her fingers curled by her side. If only she had some food she could enchant for her sister.

"I just need a minute. Alone. Please. Then I'll be back inside to congratulate him," Serafina said, chin lifting.

"This is a good thing for him, Fina. Angelo—"

"I know. I'm happy for him. Really. I just... didn't expect this."

Pamina nodded and turned to go, leaving her sister alone like she'd requested. Serafina's words and resolve surprised her. Maybe her little sister was growing up.

Stepping back outside into the cold, Pamina stumbled into something warm and solid. She looked up to find herself face to chest with Lorenzo.

Chapter 10

Get Well Soup

Lorenzo

"O h," Pamina said, colliding with Lorenzo. Her words were breathy and made him feel things he had no business feeling.

He stepped back. "My apologies, Signorina. I didn't mean to startle you."

Her eyes squinted up at him in the dark. "What are you doing out here, Signor?"

Lorenzo was thankful she couldn't see his face and how flustered he must look. Did she think he'd been spying on her and her sister? That's what it looked like.

"I came out to get the wagon hitched," he said quickly, hoping she believed him.

It was the truth anyway. He hadn't meant to overhear their private conversation. That was one discussion he definitely hadn't wanted to take part in.

"Oh. You're not staying for dessert?" she asked.

Was that disappointment in her tone? A cold gust of wind tore at their clothes. Pamina shuffled forward, the smell of her honey-scented soap hitting his nose.

The memory of her nearness in the bakery made his skin heat. He pushed the thought away, trying to keep his composure. His attraction to her was both unexpected and becoming very inconvenient.

"I'm afraid not. It will be hard to get the horse down the mountain in this darkness as it is. We can't stay any longer."

"Well, you can't travel in the dark without a lighting spell."

Lorenzo frowned at her words. "A lighting spell?"

Pamina nodded. "Yes. That's what Liliana and Dante use to travel at night."

A snort escaped him. "Yes, well, I'm afraid, I'm all out of *lighting spells*."

"Liliana can perform one for you. It might take her some time though. You might as well stay for dessert while she gets it ready for you."

"Oh, no. I couldn't impose on her. I—"

"Nonsense! You can't drive down the mountain in the pitch black. Come on, I'll go tell her. Besides Giulia would be so upset if you left before anyone tasted the pie she worked so hard on," Pamina said, turning on her heel.

She stumbled forward. Lorenzo's arm shot out, catching her. Heat flooded him at the contact. Cursing the fates for putting him in such a situation. He had no choice but to offer her his arm and lead her back.

"Thank you," she said, in that vexing breathy voice.

Pamina threaded her hand through his arm, the warmth from her hand seeping out of her glove. She glanced back at the stable.

"Should we wait for your sister?" Lorenzo asked, pausing to follow her gaze.

As much as he wanted—needed—to get inside and put some distance between them, he wasn't a complete cad. He couldn't very well leave her sister to find her way alone in the dark.

Unlike the witches and horses, Lorenzo could see perfectly at night. A feature he'd inherited from his mother.

Pamina shook her head and glanced up at him. "She'll be along shortly. She was smart and brought a lantern with her."

If she was curious as to why he didn't have one, she didn't ask. They fell into silence as he escorted her back toward the villa. Leaves and grass crunched under their boots. The wind whistled sharply through the trees behind them. The mountain air was icy cold and the thought of caffé and pie by the fire suddenly sounded very appealing.

"Are you enjoying yourself tonight, Signor?" Pamina's question broke the quiet.

"I am now," Lorenzo blurted.

Pamina stiffened beside him, a flush on her face. Lorenzo chided himself for his loose tongue. He didn't want to give her the wrong idea. As lovely as she was, he didn't need the distraction. They were only in Zamerra temporarily and when they left, it would be for good.

The front door opened as they approached. Their host, Salvatore, stood at the entrance to greet them. Lorenzo didn't like the amused gleam in his eye. Surely, there were eligible bachelors in Zamerra. Why did it seem everyone was pushing them together?

"Does this mean you're not leaving now?" Salvatore asked, opening the door wider to let them pass.

Lorenzo grunted. "It seems not. It would be rude to leave before dessert."

The man smirked. "Indeed. Especially when your sister is the one who made it."

Giulia walked up to them, the younger Rossi brother by her side. She stopped short when she saw them, a smile playing on her lips.

"Aren't you going to help Signorina Silveri with her coat, Lor?" his sister asked with a mock innocent look.

Lorenzo bit back a groan. Giulia knew exactly what she was doing and he didn't appreciate it. Shooting her a glare, he released Pamina's hand and helped her out of her coat.

His pulse quickened at the contact. The young witch's face reddened as he took the wool fabric in his arms to hang up.

"Thank you," she murmured, avoiding Lorenzo's eyes.

"Here, take this lantern." Salvatore's voice startled Lorenzo.

He turned to see the man hand his brother a lantern. With a polite nod to them, the young man left through the front door. Presumably, to go out and talk to Pamina's sister.

Giulia giggled behind him.

Everyone turned to her.

She glanced at Lorenzo, smiling. "When I was that age, you never even let me talk to boys." She turned to Pamina. "It's nice to see things have changed."

Lorenzo frowned. "I was protecting you."

Giulia walked over and squeezed his arm affectionately. "I know, but sometimes you were a little too protective."

With that, she turned and took Salvatore by the arm, as if they were old friends. "Come, Signor. I want you to be the first to try my pie. You'll give me your honest opinion, won't you?"

"Of course, Signorina." He grinned.

Their host didn't seem fazed in the least by his sister's boldness. Their voices drifted as they started walking back toward the sitting room.

Left alone with Pamina, Lorenzo was forced to offer his arm once again. This time though her gloves were off and the warmth of her hand spread up his arm. Escorting her was the proper thing to do, but the thoughts in his mind were anything but proper.

How could she affect him so when he barely knew her? Did she feel it too?

Pushing the questions aside, Lorenzo led her back to the sitting room, where everyone waited. Once she let go, he made his way to the opposite side of the room and did his best to ignore her. He was vaguely aware of them discussing the lighting spell for the horses. Hopefully, Giulia was listening to their instruction.

Light brown eyes watched him as he ate a slice of pie, but he refused to meet them. It may have been rude, but it was for the best. The wall he'd built around himself was just as much for his benefit as it was for hers.

After caffé and the 'most delicious' pumpkin pie by the fire, it was time to say goodbye. Dante and Liliana walked out with them to help set the lighting spell, which it turned out was just a giant floating orb that lit the path. The count and his wife had one of their own, but Angelo Rossi turned down Liliana's offer to make one for him. He was to stay the night with his brother and brother-in-law.

Pamina left with her mother and sisters on foot, non-magical lanterns in their hands. Lorenzo watched them disappear out of the gate before turning his attention back to the wagon cart. Giulia sat beside him, a smug smile on her face.

"Enjoying yourself, are you?" Lorenzo muttered as he led the horse forward, following the other wagons.

Giulia's grin widened. "Immensely. You can't tell me you're not. You looked pretty cozy with Pamina on your arm."

Lorenzo shushed her, glancing ahead at the others. The sound of the wagon wheels and horse hooves filled the silence.

"I told you I'm not interested, Giulia. We're here to reopen the bakery and that's it. Please stop meddling."

His sister scoffed. "I'm not meddling, Lor. Merely, pointing things out."

He turned to give her a flat look. "Well, stop."

Giulia opened her mouth to argue but stopped herself. She shook her head and looked away.

Above them, the silvery moon shone in a cloudless sky. Cold air whipped around them as they traveled down the mountain. From their position, they could see the street lamps and candles glowing from the windows in town.

It was a peaceful and beautiful sight. As much as he hated to admit it, Lorenzo could see the appeal of Zamerra. If it weren't for the fact that his *father* had chosen the little mountain town over them, he could potentially have seen himself settling there. Away from the bustle of the city.

But it was too late for that. Zamerra was not home, and it could never be.

* * *

Nearly a week had passed, and Lorenzo had put the memory of the dinner party and Pamina out of his mind. At least for the most part. With much of the old man's affairs to straighten out and Pamina busy with Giulia's baking lessons, they'd managed to keep their distance from each other in the shop.

Any day now his sister would get bored of this endeavor and tell him she was ready to leave. Leave Zamerra and all its inhabitants behind. His stomach lurched at the thought. He was ready to go, wasn't he?

Pamina's image flashed in his mind, making his heart race. There was no denying his attraction to her. That's why he remained in the back. Away from her unnerving presence. Her doe-like eyes and sweet smile.

He shut his eyes and shook his head as if that could erase her from his mind. What was the matter with him? He didn't remember simpering so much over Niccola.

You didn't love Niccola.

The wayward thought disturbed him with its implication. So, what if he hadn't felt the same *butterflies* with his ex as he was feeling now? It didn't mean anything.

It couldn't mean anything.

"Excuse me, Signor." Pamina's soft voice made him jump.

He looked up from the papers he had sprawled over the table. She smiled shyly at him and held out a plate to him.

A lopsided tart sat on the plate. It had to be one of Giulia's creations. Even with the one-on-one lessons, it was becoming clear that his sister did not inherit the old man's skills.

"Err... thank you," Lorenzo said, remembering his manners.

He took the plate from her and watched as she poured a mug of caffé for him. Without the espresso machine, Pamina had taken to brewing her own caffé for them much to Lorenzo's pleasure.

The magical drink had become a staple in the bakery and a necessary part of his routine. Where would he get such delicious enchanted caffé when he left?

Before he could take a bite, Giulia burst through the door to the little kitchen.

"I'm not feeling so well," Giulia said, a hand to her head.

"What's wrong?" Lorenzo asked, jumping to his feet.

He shared a worried look with Pamina.

"I think I need to lie down for a little bit," his sister replied.

Lorenzo helped her toward the bedroom, his chest constricting. Was it something she'd eaten? What if she was coming down with a fever like their mother?

He pushed the dark thoughts away. Giulia was young and healthy. She would be okay.

They made it to the bedroom and Lorenzo hurried over to draw back the curtain. Sunlight filtered in through the smudged glass. He squatted down to the stone fireplace to start a fire.

"This should warm up the room shortly. Do you need anything? Water?" His words were spilling out fast.

Giulia gave him a wane smile from the bed. "Don't fuss, Lor. I'm sure it's just a cold coming on or something like that."

He walked over to her and put a hand to her forehead. "Are you sure you don't have a fever?"

Her head felt cool to the touch. His shoulders sagged in relief.

She looked up at him. "No fever. I just need some rest. But, Lor, you'll have to go out there and help Pamina. There's still so much to do."

He felt his mouth drop open. "Giulia, if this is some sort of trick..."

Her nose scrunched up. "It's not, you oaf. I really don't feel well. You know I wouldn't lie about that."

They grew quiet. Memories of their mother's last days in both of their minds. Her pale face and red-rimmed eyes. The fever had stripped her of her health as well as her senses. She called out for their father, but he hadn't come. By the time they'd sent a letter to him, it had been too late.

"I'll bring you some water," Lorenzo said, pushing the memories away.

He tucked the blanket under her chin and kissed her forehead.

Giulia smiled. "You'll help her, won't you? She can't do everything alone. Besides, you were always the better baker."

Lorenzo sighed heavily and nodded. "I suppose I'll have to help her now. You get some rest."

Pamina waited outside the door with a worried frown. "Is she alright?"

Lorenzo nodded. "I think so. There's no fever. I think she just needs some rest."

"Of course. She's been working so hard. Oh, I should have sensed her symptoms sooner. I'm sorry."

The concern in her voice sounded sincere, making Lorenzo's heart warm.

"It's not your fault. I'm sure she'll be back to her usual self by morning."

Pamina nodded. "I can make her some get-well soup."

Lorenzo's eyebrow arched. "Get-well soup?"

"Yes. It's the perfect remedy for well, pretty much anything."

"Sounds delicious! Lorenzo will help you," Giulia shouted from the other side of the door.

"Oh, you don't have to do that. Unless you would like to?" Pamina asked, cheeks growing rosy.

Lorenzo ignored the urge to touch her face and gave her a curt nod. "It seems I'm at your service today, Signorina."

Pamina's eyes lit up, a smile spreading on her face. Lorenzo tried to ignore the fluttering in his stomach. How was he going to evade her now when they had to work close together in the kitchen?

Chapter 11

The Goblin's Secret

Pamina

Pamina watched as Lorenzo chopped the vegetables for the soup. Chopped them like an expert. As if he could do it in his sleep.

He paused and glanced over at her. "What is it?" His voice was gruff.

"Oh, well, I'm just surprised. Giulia told me that your mother did all the cooking until she hired someone to take over."

Lorenzo carried the cutting board to the pot and scraped the potatoes and carrots into the water. "Yes, that's true."

The vegetables plopped into the pot, filling the silence.

"Ah. You're wondering how I learned to do this?" Lorenzo's voice softened.

Pamina nodded, turning back to finish her own chopping. The strong smell of onion and roasted garlic filled her nose.

"My mother tried to give us lessons when we were younger. Giulia quickly grew bored of it, but I learned some. I used to enjoy being in the kitchen, but then I quit too."

"Why?" The question escaped her. Heat spread up her neck at her brashness.

"I mean, if you enjoyed it, why quit?"

Lorenzo turned to her, dark eyes stormy. "That was *his* thing, and I wanted nothing to do with him."

Pamina flinched at the coldness in his tone. "You mean your..." She let the words die on her tongue, knowing there was a reason the goblin didn't call the man 'father.'

The anger and hurt in Lorenzo's eyes made her heart twist. After all this time, it was clear he hadn't forgiven the man and now Signor Covelli was dead, unable to make amends. *Such a pity.*

"It seems a great shame to give up something you love just to spite someone," Pamina said, keeping her focus on the vegetables before her.

Lorenzo snorted, drawing her attention. She carried her board over to the boiling water and dumped the chopped veggies in, keenly aware of the tall brooding goblin beside her.

His presence filled the kitchen, the warmth from his body radiating around her. She could smell the caffé and sugar on his breath and that woodsy pine scent. They were so close, only a few steps and she'd be pressed against him. Against his tall, solid, muscular frame.

Face warming, she turned away and started on the spell for the soup. Lorenzo tensed up behind her.

Pamina stopped and glanced at him in concern. "What is it? What's wrong?"

Lorenzo shook his head. "What are you putting in the soup? What kind of spell?"

"I was going to put a healing spell. Something simple."

Anguish flashed across Lorenzo's face. He shut his eyes and took a deep breath, clearly in distress.

Pamina hurried to his side. "What's wrong?"

He opened his eyes, looking startled at her nearness. "I'm sorry. I just had a flashback. My mother."

Pity filled Pamina. The sorrow in his eyes made her throat tighten. "Giulia told me it was fever."

Lorenzo nodded. "Yes. We hired a witch. A healer. She promised she could heal my mother, but..." He spread his arms out.

Pamina's brow furrowed. "She should never have made that promise. Giving you false hope like that. Magic can't cure everything."

He scoffed. "Yes. I know that. Now. It was a costly lesson. Not just in coin, but... I would have given anything to save her. I still would."

Anger rolled through Pamina. How could the woman have made such a promise?

She fought the urge to hug Lorenzo. To cast a contentment spell over him to cheer him up. It was hard to see his pain, but as she knew herself, it was important to let grief run its course. It was just as she'd told him, magic couldn't fix everything.

Pamina touched his arm. His warmth spread through her. "I know there are no words of comfort I can offer that would make up for the losses you've suffered. But I am truly sorry about your mother and your father and." she paused, debating if she should say more, "your fiancée."

Lorenzo sucked in a surprised breath. "Well, it seems Giulia has told you everything about me."

Pamina shook her head. "Not everything, but I know she loves you and wants happiness for you." She shrugged a shoulder. "Isn't that what we all want for our siblings?"

Lorenzo smirked. "Your sisters are... something."

Pamina's chest tightened, her fists curled. Here she'd been pouring out her sympathy and he was making fun of her family.

"My sisters are hardworking, respectable, kind-hearted, and

brilliant. I won't allow you or anyone for that matter to speak ill of them." Her voice quavered with emotion.

Lorenzo's eyes widened. "Woah. I didn't mean to upset you, Pamina. I think your sisters are lovely. I would never speak ill of them or you," he said with an earnest look.

Pamina. He'd called her by her first name and the realization sent a wave of shock through her. Though she hadn't given him permission to use it so familiarly, she found she liked it. Liked the way it sounded on his lips.

He studied her as if waiting to see how she would respond. Suddenly the kitchen felt much too warm and much too small. The soup bubbled behind them, interrupting the quiet. The savory smell of the vegetables and herbs wafted around the room.

"Uh.... is anyone coming with that water?" Giulia called from the back room, breaking the spell.

Lorenzo blew out a breath and turned to the door. "Coming!"

Pamina watched as he hurriedly poured water into a glass and retreated to the bedroom. The kitchen felt colder without his presence. Her heart hammered loudly in her ears.

Was this the feeling she'd been waiting for, for so long? Was this love?

She pushed the silly thought away. Lorenzo was her employer and apart from his forwardness that day, he'd shown nothing but polite indifference to her.

Then why does it feel like something more?

Pamina busied herself with the contentment spell. Keeping busy always helped. She closed her eyes and focused on the magic buzzing through her. Eyes tightly clenched, she slowed her breathing and envisioned the magic swirling into the soup.

Strength. Rest. Healing.

She pictured Giulia eating the soup, the sickness in her body leaving. Her face glowing with good health.

Opening her eyes, Pamina turned around and cast the spell into the pot. The broth splashed up along the sides, nearly spilling out. She lowered the heat and stirred before putting the lid back on.

The smell of the soup made her mouth water. It was nearly lunchtime. Normally, she and Giulia ate something quick before returning to work, but with the young woman sick in bed, would it just be her and Lorenzo? Would he eat with her or disappear into the back?

It would be a while before the soup was ready, so Pamina glanced around for something else to make. The glass displays were filled with Giulia's pastries and cookies they'd been making. Some of them looked good enough to sell, but most of them lacked the finesse Signor Covelli's treats had.

"How long until the soup is done?" Lorenzo's voice startled her.

She turned to see him reappear, his giant frame filling the doorway.

"Oh, it's going to need a few hours," she replied.

He frowned. "Right. Well, Giulia's requested a full lunch today. Ravioli and bread so why don't you take a break while I run out? I can help you finish whatever you need to after we eat."

Pamina glanced around the bakery. "Oh, Signora Giamatti makes the best bread. We can stop there on the way to the ristorante. They'll have ravioli."

A hesitant look flashed on Lorenzo's face. Pamina flushed. She hadn't meant to invite herself along, but the thought of walking with him and getting to know him better was enticing.

Did he not feel the same?

"Or would you rather I stay here and keep an eye on Giulia?" Pamina asked.

"You don't need to stay and babysit me! Please go. I need some peace and quiet, anyway," Giulia yelled.

Pamina bit back a smile.

Lorenzo rolled his eyes and turned to her. "I can ready the wagon then."

"You don't have to do that for me. A walk sounds nice actually," Pamina said, glancing out the front window.

She might regret it once she stepped out into the cold, but some time out of the bakery with Lorenzo by her side filled her with excitement. She couldn't wait to show him around Zamerra.

"After you then, Signorina Silveri," he said with a polite bow.

Pamina frowned. What happened to him calling her by her first name? Was it back to business now?

Dismissing the thoughts, she walked to the door to retrieve her coat and gloves. Lorenzo stood behind her, waiting to get his gear as well. Pamina buttoned up her coat and pulled the hood over her head. She felt Lorenzo's eyes on her as she put on her gloves.

She met his gaze, her breath catching. His lips were pressed into a thin line, but his dark eyes were hooded.

He looked away first, something like repulsion on his face. Pamina's heart sank. Was he repulsed by her? Is that why he stared at her? She turned away so he wouldn't see her hurt. For a minute, she'd believed he'd found her as attractive as she found him.

Swallowing the lump in her throat, she tried to put the thoughts aside. She could do nothing about her size and if he couldn't accept her for how she was, then she'd have to move past it.

Suddenly a walk with him trying to hide his disgust didn't sound so appealing. She glanced back at the pot of soup simmering on the stove. Perhaps she should stay.

"Ready?" Lorenzo's gruff voice broke through her thoughts.

He was already dressed and ready. Head held high, she nodded and waited for him to lead the way. Pamina followed him outside.

Cold air struck her face as they began walking. Lorenzo motioned her forward and kept his distance. Their boots slapped loudly against the cobblestoned streets. Voices and wagon wheels drifted from the next street.

People waved to them as they passed, pausing with autumn wreaths and garlands in their hands. Some stopped to point and whisper. Pamina glanced back at Lorenzo, wondering what was going through his mind. He stared straight ahead, ignoring her.

His actions stung. She thought they'd had a moment in the bakery, but it turned out she was wrong. Chimney smoke billowed into the bright blue sky and savory and sweet smells clashed together. The townsfolk were pausing their work to have lunch.

They made it to the bread maker's shop and stood in line. The smell of freshly baked bread and caffé made Pamina's stomach rumble. It wasn't her special brew, but it still smelled delicious.

The people ahead of them turned to look at their approach, surprise shining on their faces.

Pamina gave them a warm smile. "Good day," she said.

"Good day, Signorina. Signor," Signora Savelli replied, her eyebrow arched and lips pursed.

The older woman, now retired, had been the town's matchmaker. She'd been outright rude to Alessia and hadn't approved of her marrying the count. Serafina sent rats to crawl up her skirts in retaliation. Since then, the woman hadn't uttered anything but compliments about the Silveri girls.

Signora Savelli turned her attention to Lorenzo. "We've been wondering when we would see you and your sister in town again. Your sister is quite the shopper, isn't she? We had no idea Signor Covelli had left such a fortune—"

"He left nothing, but the bakery, Signora. I'd hardly call that a fortune. Everything we've earned, we've earned ourselves," Lorenzo cut her off.

He was practically snarling. Pamina frowned at the older woman, willing her to keep her mouth shut.

Of course, that was too much to ask of the busybody.

Signora Savelli clucked her tongue, refusing to be waylaid. "Such a shame about poor Signor Covelli. His was the best bakery in town, you know. Such a shame it's closed now."

"It's only temporary, Signora. Signor Bartoli and his sister plan to reopen in time for the Harvest Festival," Pamina told her.

The woman's eyes gleamed. "Oh?"

Before she could pester them with questions, a voice called from behind them. Pamina turned to see Stefano walking their way.

"Signorina Silveri! I've been hoping to see you in town. You didn't come to the reception," the young man said, eyes flickering to Lorenzo.

Stefano stepped forward and took Pamina's hand, ignoring Lorenzo completely. "Come have lunch with me, Signorina."

A few gasps sounded and Signora Savelli gave a loud 'harrumph'. Heat spread across Pamina's skin. Everyone was watching them.

Chapter 12

The Other Man

Lorenzo

Lorenzo watched as the golden-haired man stepped around him to grab Pamina's hand. Anger rippled through him. Who was this man? Why was he holding her hand so possessively?

He had the sudden urge to snatch her out of his grasp. It was just concern, he told himself, that made him react so. Not jealousy. This man was trouble. He could sense it.

"I'm afraid Signorina Silveri already has lunch plans," he heard himself say.

Gasps echoed from the crowd of onlookers. The older woman behind Pamina looked as if she was going to faint.

Pamina's cheeks reddened.

The man released her hand and whipped to Lorenzo. His eyes narrowed as he took Lorenzo in, green skin and pointed ears. A look of disgust flashed across his features. It was a look Lorenzo was more than familiar with.

"I'm sorry?" The words sounded more like a challenge than a question.

Lorenzo bit back a harsh laugh. Did he really think he was a match for Lorenzo's size and strength? The man's head barely came to Lorenzo's chest.

He felt his lips pull back into a cold smile. "Forgive me. I spoke too fast it seems. Signorina Silveri already has plans for lunch," he enunciated each word slowly.

Rage lit the man's face.

"Yes, I'm sorry, Signor Rivaldi. We're bringing lunch back to Signorina Bartoli in the bakery. She's feeling unwell, you see. Perhaps another time?" Pamina's soft voice rang behind them.

Lorenzo's gaze snapped to her. *Another time?* Did she actually like this green-eyed fool?

Swallowing his disappointment, he straightened his shoulders and looked at the man.

Signor Rivaldi, as she'd called him, turned toward her, his back to Lorenzo. "I see. You're working in the bakery now?"

Pamina nodded.

The man stepped closer to her. "Unchaperoned?" he asked loudly.

Lorenzo felt his jaw tighten. What was he implying? The crowd tittered. No doubt, storing this tidbit of gossip to spread around town.

"Oh, no. I'm working with his sister. We've been preparing the bakery for the Harvest Festival. It's just business," Pamina said quickly.

Just business. The words shouldn't have stung so. She'd spoken truly, but Lorenzo couldn't help but feel disappointed. He thought there was something growing between them. It appeared he was wrong.

"Hmm. I find this a little concerning, but I trust Signor Bartoli knows his place," the man said, glancing back at Lorenzo with a raised brow.

His threat made Lorenzo's hackles rise. It implied much more than impropriety. As a half-goblin, in a society that favored humans, Lorenzo had *learned his place* many times over.

"I appreciate your concern, Signor, but Signor Bartoli has been nothing but professional and proper. And I am not one to be taken in so easily by *any* man. Do not insult him or me so," Pamina said with a haughty sniff.

Lorenzo smiled. The gentle witch had a bite when provoked and he loved her all the more for it.

Loved?

He pushed the thought away quickly. It was just business, as she said.

"Please, Signorina, I meant no offense. It's *him* I don't trust," Signor Rivaldi said, eyes narrowed on Lorenzo again.

"Come on. Move up!" someone shouted behind them, breaking the tension.

Fighting the urge to square off with Pamina's admirer, Lorenzo ignored his glare and gave Pamina a pointed look.

"Excuse us, Signor Rivaldi," she said as she moved to follow the line of people.

The man nodded at her and turned his attention back to Lorenzo. His lip curled, but he didn't say anything else as he sauntered away. It didn't matter. Lorenzo had learned early on that there was nothing he could say to change someone's mind once it was made up.

Some people could accept him and some could not. That was life.

Following Pamina, he tried to put the encounter out of his mind. Did this man have a history with Pamina? Was she actually fond of him?

He wanted to ask her all this and more but knew he couldn't.

Knows his place... The man's words echoed in his mind.

Yes. He knew his place and it wasn't in Zamerra with

Pamina. He glanced at the beautiful witch. If Signor Rivaldi is what she liked, then he had never stood a chance with her anyway. It was better that way.

Is it though?

After getting their bread, they made their way to the ristorante for the ravioli. Neither he nor Pamina said a word, their steps filling the silence.

The fresh bread wrapped in the thin cloth filled his nose, making Lorenzo's stomach rumble. He was ready to get the food and return to the bakery. To the warmth. It had nothing to do with having the beautiful baking witch all to himself.

As much as he didn't want the bakery, Pamina's presence made it much more bearable. Her bright smile and soft curves would haunt him in his dreams forever.

Lorenzo glanced at her. She met his stare with a questioning look in her brown eyes. The cold made her cheeks rosy, and it took him great effort to tear his eyes away.

The walk back to the shop was excruciating. A heavy tension hung between them and all the ease they'd developed earlier had been erased. Had he upset her when he stepped in? Was she secretly wishing she was with that golden-haired fop instead of stuck with him?

That thought distressed him more than he'd like to admit.

"I'm sorry about Signor Rivaldi," Pamina finally spoke, interrupting his thoughts.

Lorenzo frowned. "A close friend of yours?" He couldn't hide the edge in his tone.

Pamina shook her head. "He's the tailor's son. We used to go to school together when I was young, but I wouldn't say we're close."

"Ah," Lorenzo replied, falling quiet.

Questions raced in his mind, but he wouldn't ask them out loud. Her relationship with the *tailor's son* was none of his business. Besides, he'd be leaving Zamerra as soon as Giulia was ready, and he'd never see the man or Pamina again.

For some reason, the thought of never seeing her anymore dampened his spirits.

"He didn't mean any offense. He was just a concerned friend."

Lorenzo snorted. "I don't think *friendship* is what he wants, Signorina."

Pamina stiffened, red creeping along her face. So, she did like the man. That left a bitter taste in Lorenzo's mouth. His fingers curled into fists.

He forced a smile. "My apologies. I shouldn't have spoken so boldly. I'm sure he's a perfect gentleman. Best wishes to you both."

Lorenzo cringed at his own words. What was he saying? *Best wishes?*

Pamina looked down at her boots, steps faltering. "Thank you," she said softly.

They continued to the bakery, both silent.

Warmth enveloped them as they stepped inside, and the garlicky and basil smell of the soup filled the little shop. Hands full, Lorenzo walked to the front counter and set down the container of ravioli and wrapped bread.

"I'm going to go check on Giulia. Please help yourself to the food. You don't need to wait for us," he told Pamina as she hung up her coat and peeled off her gloves.

She nodded in return, her eyes not meeting his.

Lorenzo frowned. He didn't like this chasm growing between them, but perhaps it was safer that way.

Turning away, he tried to push all thoughts of the witch out of his mind. He knocked on the bedroom door and waited for Giulia to respond.

No answer came. He cracked the door open and peeked inside. His sister was sound asleep, snoring gently.

A smile spread on his lips. She looked too peaceful to stir. They could save her some pasta and bread for later. Perhaps the soup would be ready by the time she woke up.

With Giulia sound asleep, that meant he would be left alone to eat with Pamina. His stomach fluttered with nerves. He didn't like this strange sensation that had come over him. He'd never been one to be taken in by a pretty face. So, why did the witch have such an effect on him?

Dismissing the questions racing in his mind, Lorenzo made his way to the front of the shop. Pamina stood at one of the little tables by the chiminea, plating ravioli.

The sunlight streamed in, highlighting her profile. Her flawless tan skin and shiny loose curls. The dark green blouse and brown skirt hugged her body so perfectly.

She looked up at Lorenzo and smiled. "How is she?"

"Hmm?"

Her brow furrowed. "Giulia? How is she doing?"

Lorenzo shook away the wayward thoughts. "Oh, she's sleeping. I didn't want to wake her."

Pamina nodded. "Good. She needs rest. I can set aside a plate for her for when she wakes."

She gestured to the empty chair. "Do you want to join me?"

It was an innocent offer, but it made Lorenzo tense up. Eating lunch with Pamina at the tiny table felt too intimate. Too dangerous.

"Thank you for the offer, but I'm afraid I have too much work to finish in the back. With Giulia sick, there's no reason for you to stay the whole day. Enjoy your lunch and then you're free to go. I can drive you up the mountain when you're ready."

Pamina gaped at him, a look of hurt flashing in her eyes.

The look sent a spear of pain through him. Didn't she want to go?

"Oh, I'll pay you for the whole day though. If that's your concern," he added quickly.

She snapped her mouth shut and shook her head. "I'm not concerned about that, Signor." She sounded insulted.

Lorenzo blinked in confusion. He hadn't meant to upset her.

Unsure of what else to say, he nodded and started to turn away.

"Don't you want your plate?" Pamina asked.

He walked over to her and took the steaming plate from her hands. Their fingers brushed briefly. The contact sent a shiver down his back. For a minute, Lorenzo imagined tossing the plate aside and pulling Pamina into his arms. Leaning down and capturing her lips with his. Bodies pressed together.

"Thank you," he finally replied, unable to shake the gravelly sound in his voice.

Her large brown eyes flicked to his lips, making his skin heat.

It took all his strength to turn and walk away from her. His pulse quickened and his boots slapped loudly against the wood floor. The smell of the pumpkin ravioli and fresh bread filled his nostrils. He bit back a groan. He was hungry, but not for pasta.

Banishing all thoughts and images of the beautiful witch, he took a seat in the back kitchen and started eating. The stacks of paper before him caught his eye. He'd lied when he told her there was more work. He'd finished it that morning but couldn't bring himself to stay and have lunch with her.

It was rude of him, he knew. Giulia would be furious when she found out. He wasn't exactly proud of his actions either. The thought of the poor witch out there eating alone made him shake his head.

It's better this way.

After finishing his plate and another mug of Pamina's special caffé, he drummed his fingers on the table and sighed.

A soft knock startled him.

"Yes?" he asked.

Pamina pushed the door open and peeked in. "Are you sure you don't want me to finish anything before I leave? I don't mind working alone."

Lorenzo stood, chair scraping against the wood. "No. That's not necessary. Thank you. Let me check on Giulia first, then I'll ready the wagon for us."

"Oh, you don't have to do that, Signor. I'm fine with walking," she said, eyes darting away.

"It's quite a walk up the mountain."

Pamina shrugged. "I don't mind."

"Are you sure?"

Her eyes narrowed at him. "As surprising as you might find it, I'm used to walking."

There was a sharpness in her tone. Had he said something offensive?

"As you wish, Signorina," he replied with a grunt.

He walked over to escort her out. It was the least he could do if she wouldn't let him drive her home. Maybe the thought of being seen with him in town is what upset her.

Wouldn't want Signor Rivaldi to see them again.

Pamina moved away from the door as he joined her.

A hesitant look crept on her face before she pressed on. "Before I go, I wanted to ask you if I could have some time off. Just a day."

A day off? *Perhaps another time.* The words she'd spoken to the tailor's son echoed in his mind. She wanted a day off to see *him*.

"I've been promising my sister, Fiorella, that we'll have a

sisters' day, but it's been hard to find the time," Pamina continued.

Guilt struck him. Here he'd been envisioning her running off to meet that golden-haired swine. Before his mind could conjure images of them together, he pushed the thoughts away.

Lorenzo stopped at the front door and looked at her. "A day off? We've been working you too much, haven't we?"

Pamina grabbed her coat and gloves, eyes darting away. They'd never gone over her terms when she'd started. Mostly because he had been trying to avoid her at all costs and Giulia wasn't one to bother with formalities.

He shook his head, frowning. "Of course, we have. I should have been more aware. Of course, you can have a day off. You can have a week off if that's what you wish."

"Oh, no!" Pamina blurted, face flushing. "I mean, I don't need a whole week off. With the festival only weeks away, there's still much to do. Unless... you would like me to take off?"

"No," he replied quickly.

"I mean, we still need you here. But any day you like, you may have it," he added.

Pamina smiled. "Thank you. Oh, and the soup should be ready soon. One bowl should be enough to heal her. I'll be back in the morning to check on her and finish the pies for the festival."

"I'll make sure there's room in the storeroom to keep them fresh," Lorenzo replied.

With a final wave, Pamina left.

The bakery was silent. Distress filled Lorenzo at the thought of her leaving even for a day. It was foolishness though. He had no right to monopolize her time. Besides, when they left Zamerra, he'd be leaving her behind along with it. Maybe the more times he repeated it, the easier it would be to accept.

Chapter 13

Sisters' Day

Pamina

With Pamina's special soup, Giulia made a quick recovery. Though Pamina was happy to see her back to health the next day, she couldn't help but wish for more time alone with Lorenzo. If only they had more time, maybe then she could figure the grumpy goblin out.

There were times when she thought she saw desire burning in his dark eyes, but his actions said otherwise. The memory of him and Stefano flashed in her mind.

Best wishes to you both, Lorenzo had told her.

Truthfully, she hadn't given Stefano another thought since Lorenzo's arrival. She would have much rather spent her time with Signor Covelli's heir, getting to know him better and she thought he'd felt the same about her. Yet when they'd had the chance to sit and eat together, he'd fled.

As if the mere thought of being in her presence was repugnant. Even now, he hid himself in the back, only coming out to pour himself a quick cup of her caffé before scurrying out of sight.

Giulia sighed, pulling Pamina's attention away from the back door.

The young woman had been unnaturally quiet that morning. Not her usual bubbly self.

"Are you sure you're feeling alright? I can make more soup. Or something else if you like," Pamina said as she watched Giulia frost a cookie half-heartedly.

Giulia sighed again and set down her knife. "I'm fine. I just..." She shook her head. "I didn't expect to end up here. In this place. Frosting cookies of all things."

She snorted and set down the half-finished pumpkin-shaped treat. "A few months ago, I was picking out wedding invitations and tablecloths." Her voice turned wobbly.

Pamina's heart twisted. She hated to see her friend in such distress.

Giulia sniffed and looked at Pamina with watery eyes. "Oh, you must think I'm terribly shallow. I don't care about the tablecloths. Or any of that stuff. I mean I always dreamed of a big, fancy wedding, but honestly, if Riccardo had asked me to elope, I would have said yes."

Her forehead creased as she stared at the cookie on the plate before her. "I know it's pathetic, but I miss him."

Pamina laid a hand on top of Giulia's. "It's not pathetic at all. I think it's perfectly understandable. Is there anything I can do to help?"

Another pie, perhaps. She could mix in a mending spell. Something that would help her friend get through this heartbreak. Sugar made everything better.

Giulia gave her a wry smile. "Conjure up the perfect man? One that comes with no meddling family, perhaps?"

"I'm afraid my magic is limited to healing food. Besides, I don't think a perfect man exists."

Giulia shrugged. "No, but my Riccardo was pretty damn close."

She gave Pamina a sheepish look. "Excuse my language."

Pamina snorted. "Trust me, I've heard much worse. From the mouth of my fifteen-year-old sister no less."

Giulia grinned. "Serafina? A girl after my own heart."

"You should come to her birthday next week. You and your brother."

Hopefully, Serafina wouldn't mind that she'd invited them. A party and good food would be just the thing to cheer up poor Giulia. Though the thought of Lorenzo in her home made her turn crimson. What would he think of the villa? Of her family?

"Oh! That would be lovely. Thank you. What should we bring her? And don't say 'just bring yourselves.' Shopping for the perfect present is the best part."

Pamina smiled at her friend's enthusiasm. "Well, she loves animals and nature. Though, come to think of it, I think she's secretly becoming fonder of finer things."

Giulia squealed. "A dress! Every young woman needs a fancy dress that makes her feel like a queen."

Pamina didn't think *every* was accurate, but she wasn't about to argue. Not when it was the first time the young woman had smiled that day.

"Oh, but is there anyone in town that can make a dress in such a short time?" Giulia held a finger to her chin in thought.

"Well, we have a tailor."

Giulia's nose scrunched up. "Yes, I've been by there but haven't had time to go in."

"Signora Rivaldi, the tailor's wife, is the most skilled dressmaker in Zamerra."

Even as she said the words, Pamina regretted them. Going to the tailor's shop meant she would have to see Stefano again. What if he asked her to dine with him again?

Lorenzo's words rang in her ears. *Best wishes to you both.*

"Then we must go. After we've finished here, of course." Giulia said sullenly, glancing at the many rows of cookies cooling on the rack.

Pamina had never seen the young woman work so quickly. In no time, the cookies were ready and placed in the back cooler to keep them fresh. Once they'd finished, Giulia ran to the back to let Lorenzo know where they were heading. Pamina strained to hear his response but could hear nothing.

The air was crisp and cool outside. People milled around, everyone busily preparing for the upcoming festival.

"Should we bring some lunch back for your brother while we're out?" Pamina asked, breaking the silence.

Giulia, who'd been waving to the crowd of onlookers, turned to Pamina with a sly grin. "That's very thoughtful of you. I'm sure he'll appreciate anything you bring him. I'm sure you've noticed how he can't seem to keep his eyes off of you."

A harsh laugh nearly escaped Pamina. It seemed Giulia had misread her brother's reactions just as she had.

She must have made a face because Giulia frowned. "What is it? He hasn't offended you, has he?"

"No. Of course not. It's just... he's difficult to read," Pamina admitted with a shrug.

Giulia stopped in the middle of the street, a serious look on her face now. "Do you like my brother?"

Heat swarmed up Pamina's neck. Giulia's question stunned her. "What?"

The young woman smiled. "I thought so. He likes you too."

At this, Pamina did laugh. "No. I don't think so."

Giulia grabbed her hand, squeezing it tightly. "Trust me, he does. He just... he's been hurt before. The fiancée I told you about. She left him for another man. There have been very few people in his life that haven't let him down. I think that's why he keeps himself so guarded."

Pamina's chest tightened. It was just as she suspected. He was hurting, but the question was, did he want to heal? Sometimes holding onto the bitterness was easier than the work it took to get better.

"I'll talk to him," Giulia said with a satisfied smile.

"No! Please. I mean..."

Giulia winked. "Don't worry. Unlike some families, I don't meddle. At least not too much."

With that, she threaded her arm through Pamina's and continued on. They made it to the tailor's, Pamina's head buzzing with thoughts of Lorenzo as they stepped inside.

The brass bell above the door announced their arrival. Signor Rivaldi, the tailor, looked up from the giant cutting table in the middle of the shop.

"Good afternoon, Signorinas!" he said, setting aside his shears and the fabric he'd been working on.

They returned his greeting in unison. The shop was bigger than the bakery and smelled faintly like cinnamon and candle wax.

Pamina took in the wooden shelves of fabric rolls and bolts. Wool, silk, cotton, and linen were spread out and organized by color.

Giulia pointed to a wooden mannequin that stood in the storefront window. It wore a soft pink silk dress that looked much too fancy for the little mountain town.

"Do you think your sister would like something like that?" Giulia asked, giving the dress a long look.

Signor Rivaldi, abandoning his work, walked over to them and smiled. "Oh, that's a fine dress for any occasion."

Pamina tried to picture Serafina in it with her auburn curls and brown skin. It would complement her features quite nicely, but it didn't look like a dress her sister would pick out for herself.

She shook her head at Giulia's questioning glance.

"Can we see some similar fabric? Perhaps gold?" Giulia asked the tailor.

Pamina followed as Signor Rivaldi led them further into the shop. Thankfully, there was no sign of Stefano, and she could relax. She did her best to answer Giulia's questions and offer her input, but her mind drifted back to their earlier conversation.

He likes you.

Could it really be true? A spark of hope filled her at the thought.

The memory of Lorenzo fussing over his sister warmed her. It was obvious he loved and adored Giulia just as much as she loved and adored her own sisters. What would it be like to have him fussing over her so? For a brief moment, she let the fantasy play.

Lorenzo at her bedside, nursing her back to health. Not that she couldn't heal herself, but it would be nice to be the patient, for a change.

To have someone care for her so deeply. A partner. A soulmate.

An aching filled her chest. She clenched her eyes shut and pushed away the thought.

After leaving the shop with the promise to return once the dress was ready, they made their way back to the bakery. Pamina did her best to concentrate on the work at hand but found her gaze drifting to the closed door. What would it take to get Lorenzo to open it for her?

* * *

The next afternoon Pamina found herself quite distracted as she sat at her sister's kitchen table, a mug between her hands.

It had been a long time since they'd all been together without the men. Franny, Alessia's house elf, sat with them, sipping loudly from her tiny mug. Pamina glanced at the tray of bomboloni that was quickly being devoured. They were from the same batch she'd made with Giulia earlier that morning. Much to her delight, Lorenzo had come out to try them and say good morning.

His handsome face flashed in her mind. Before her thoughts could drift further, she pushed them away and renewed her focus on the conversation she'd been missing.

Today wasn't a day to think about him or men in general. Today was the day they'd reserved for some sisterly bonding at Alessia's villa. Besides, she didn't want any of her sisters to pick up on her confusing feelings.

Liliana waved a hand in front of her and frowned. "Hello? Pamina, what is this I hear about you going to the tailor's to see Stefano?"

Everyone fell quiet, their eyes on Pamina.

"I don't know what you're talking about," Pamina replied, setting down her mug.

Liliana leaned forward in her chair. "Please tell me you're not entertaining the idea of Stefano Rivaldi. You know he's nothing but trouble."

Pamina's face grew warm under her sister's judgmental stare. "Liliana, I have no idea what you're talking about. I haven't made any plans with Stefano."

"Good. Stay away from him," Liliana retorted.

A huff escaped Pamina. "I'm not some dog you can order around, Liliana."

Serafina snorted, watching the exchange with a wicked smile. She was the one who usually bickered with Liliana.

Fiorella and Alessia watched too, concern shining in their eyes. Even little Franny had stopped drinking to stare, eyebrows raised in surprise.

Liliana's lip curled. "I'm trying to protect you, Pamina. You are too trusting of people."

Her sister's words rang in her ears. Deep down she knew Liliana meant well, but she didn't appreciate her sister's insinuation that she was a naïve dimwit.

Alessia cleared her throat. "You've shared your concerns, Liliana. That's enough. Pamina can make up her own mind."

Pamina shot her an appreciative look. This was supposed to be sisters' day and she didn't want to fight.

Liliana sat back in her chair and shook her head. "With you as contessa, Alessia, everyone is watching our family now. Even more so than before. We can't afford any... embarrassments."

Pamina's mouth dropped open. She felt the sting of her sister's words. *Embarrassment.*

"When have I ever brought embarrassment to our family? I believe that role has been reserved for you and Serafina." The words tumbled out of her before she could stop them.

Fiorella gasped.

"Hey! Don't bring me into this," Serafina snapped.

Liliana scowled at Pamina. "Oh, and what have I done to embarrass *you?*"

Alessia spread her hands in a placating manner. "Enough of this. Stop. None of us have any reason to be ashamed or embarrassed."

That should have been where the argument ended, but Pamina couldn't help but continue.

"I've always supported you, Liliana. Always. Even when you've been a downright..."

Liliana's eyes narrowed. "Go on. Say it. I know you've been dying to. There's no man here you need to impress."

Pamina's temper flared. "How dare you! Is that what you think of me? That my only aim in life is to impress some man?"

"Stop! This is supposed to be sisters' day and all you can do is fight!" Fiorella exclaimed, tears welling in her eyes.

With that, she bolted from the table and ran outside. Pamina's heart sank.

Serafina turned her fierce glare on Pamina and Liliana. "Now see what you've done? I hope you're proud of yourselves."

She shook her head at them before chasing after her younger sister. Alessia frowned at them.

Liliana turned to Pamina, a stricken look on her face. "I'm sorry. I didn't mean that, Pamina."

"I'm sorry too."

Alessia leaned forward and took each of their hands. She sighed. "I may be contessa now, but I'm your sister first and foremost, and I am proud of each one of you. I hope you both know that."

Pamina's heart warmed at her sister's words. In many ways, Alessia had been more of a mother to them than Mama at times.

"I should probably go and apologize to Serafina and Fiorella," Pamina said as she withdrew her hand from Alessia's.

Liliana nodded. "I'll come with you."

They threw on their coats and found the girls sitting outside on the covered swing. Alessia followed them.

"We're sorry for fighting, Ella. Won't you please come inside?" Pamina started.

"We promise no more fighting. Why don't we start a card game?" Liliana suggested, arms spread in a pacifying gesture.

Fiorella smiled at this and rose to her feet. She rushed to hug them both, Serafina and Alessia piling in after her.

"Let's play Queens," Serafina said, voice muffled.

Liliana snorted. "Only if you promise not to cheat."

"I do not cheat!"

"You do so. I've seen you exchange very suspicious looks with Lucia when you play," Liliana insisted.

Alessia released them to put her hands on her hips. "What? Fina! You can't use the cat to cheat at cards."

"No more fighting! You promised," Fiorella shouted above them.

Properly chastised by the youngest, they all fell silent and headed back inside. Pamina smiled at her sisters. Whoever she ended up with would have to accept and love them just as they were. A certain dark-eyed man sprang to mind, but she knew better than to get her hopes up. If he cared for her, as Giulia insisted, he needed to show her.

Chapter 14

The Pie

Lorenzo

"Giulia, what are you doing? We're supposed to be at the bakery already. Are you feeling well?"

Lorenzo knocked on his sister's door once more, listening for her answer. Growing concerned, he turned the knob and peered inside.

Giulia stood by her mirror, pinning her hair up. She turned to him with a frown. "I'm feeling fine, thank you. But I won't be joining you in the bakery today."

"You won't be joining me in the bakery?"

Giulia turned back to finish her hair, her eyes meeting his in the mirror. "That's right."

"And why is that? Dare I hope you've decided we should sell the bakery after all?"

"Of course not!"

Lorenzo sighed and rubbed his forehead. "Then why won't you be accompanying me today?"

Giulia smiled at him. "I have business in town. The dresses I've ordered are nearly finished, and I want to see them. Now before you have a fit, I'll be fine on my own. Zamerra is perfectly safe."

"I see. So, while you're out gallivanting about town, what am I supposed to tell Pa—Signorina Silveri?"

His sister turned to him with a triumphant smile. "I'm sure she won't mind my absence at all. You're the better baker anyway, Lor. We both know that."

Another sigh escaped him. "Giulia, you do realize that you're putting us in a... delicate situation? There is the young woman's reputation to uphold."

Giulia snorted. "Oh, please. Times have changed, brother. I don't think Pamina cares about such outdated notions."

A sly grin spread on her face. "I'll be in by lunchtime. Or so. Plenty of time for you two to figure out what is you both want."

Lorenzo huffed. "You promised you wouldn't meddle."

His sister lifted her chin. "And this is me keeping that promise, silly. With me out of the way, you'll have her all to yourself."

"You are the most vexing sister. I assume there's no changing your mind on this matter, is there?"

Ignoring his question, Giulia blew him a kiss and put her coat on. Lorenzo followed her out of the room, giving her instructions to stay away from any dark alleys or suspicious characters. She waved off his brotherly advice and made her way downstairs to inquire about a driver.

Lorenzo bit back a curse as he watched his sister board the wagon and head off down the street in the opposite direction. He shoved his hands into his coat pockets and started walking toward the bakery.

A giant mug of Pamina's brew was just what he needed. Despite his sister's confidence that the baking witch wouldn't mind being alone with him, Lorenzo wasn't so sure that was the case.

They'd barely spoken since the day they'd walked to the ristorante together, but the memory of seeing her with the tailor's son burned in the back of Lorenzo's mind. Had she ever gone to meet him?

Did she prefer him over Lorenzo? Why wouldn't she? All questions he couldn't ask her and needed to put away.

It was none of his business. His business, it seemed, was to fill in for his sister and help Pamina prepare the bakery for reopening. Though the idea of having something to do besides hiding in the back was appealing, his stomach felt funny at the prospect of spending time with the witch. He'd been perfectly happy with the walls he'd built until he'd met her.

The bakery was cold and dark when he arrived. Thankfully, Pamina seemed to be running late which gave him time to get more kindling and start the fire. He'd just got a nice blaze going when the door opened.

Pamina walked in, a basket in hand. She looked surprised to see him.

"Good morning," Lorenzo greeted her as he brushed his hands together.

"Good morning, Signor," she returned politely, glancing around the empty shop.

Lorenzo watched as she set the basket down on one of the tables and hung up her coat. She tucked her gloves into one of the pockets and turned back to face him.

He was vaguely aware he was staring at her but couldn't look away. Her hair was plaited back, her eyes bright, and her body encased in a simple brown dress and cream-colored apron.

Kindling crackled in the chiminea, filling the awkward silence.

"Is Giulia not feeling well?" Pamina asked with a furrowed brow.

Her lips were downturned in concern and Lorenzo had the frightful urge to kiss them. Shoving the thought aside, he shook his head, trying to compose himself. He never should have come.

"What's wrong? Should I make some more soup? Or I can get my sister and Dante. They could make her a healing tonic. Does she have a fever?"

Her words rushed around him making him blink in confusion. He shook his head again.

"Lorenzo, you're starting to scare me. Please. What's wrong with Giulia?" Pamina's voice wavered.

Lorenzo. It was the first time he'd heard her use his first name, and the wave of delight it caused was entirely unseemly.

Pamina stepped toward him, worry shining in her eyes. That's when he realized he hadn't answered her. Worse, he'd caused her pain.

"Giulia is fine. Forgive me. I seem to be somewhere else this morning." His words came out clipped and sharper than he'd meant.

Relief flashed across the witch's face. "*Santo Cielo.* You scared me."

"I didn't mean to scare you, Pamina." His voice softened.

Her gaze snapped to his. The air between them was charged with... well, charged with *something.* But he didn't think it was magic. Truthfully, he had no idea what was happening. How could she make him feel this way with a mere look?

"Giulia is not here," he heard himself speak, interrupting the silence.

Pamina arched an eyebrow at him. Lorenzo chided himself for such a moronic, obvious statement, but it was an anchor, steeling him before he could get swept away in his feelings.

"She said she had some dresses to check on or something. She should be here by lunchtime. I'm afraid this means you're stuck with me this morning. My apologies in advance."

Amusement flickered on the witch's face. "What are you apologizing for? For your sister's absence or your presence?"

Lorenzo snorted. "Both, I suppose. In any case, should I say something inappropriate or behave offensively, you have your apology up front."

Pamina gaped at him. "Are you planning to be offensive, Signor?"

Heat spread across Lorenzo's skin. He was making a mess of this already.

"No, of course not! I didn't mean... I would never... er, what's in the basket?"

Turning her attention to said basket, Pamina smiled. "I've brought some more pumpkin puree to make more pies today."

"You must have a lot of pumpkins in your garden," Lorenzo said, thankful, they'd moved past his blunder.

Her eyes met his. "They won't stop springing up."

Before he could question such an odd answer, she turned back to her basket and pulled something out. A carafe of her special brew.

"Ah. I was counting on your caffé. Thank you," Lorenzo said.

The smile she gave him made something crack inside him. It was such an open smile, full of joy and hope. Things he hadn't felt in a very long time.

"Will you be coming to my sister's party next week?" Pamina's question startled him.

He frowned. "A party?"

Her smile faltered. "Yes. She's turning sixteen. Giulia is having a dress made for her. I'm sorry. I thought Giulia had extended my invitation to you. Will you come?"

Lorenzo's heart skipped. She'd never asked something of him and as badly as he wanted to say yes, he knew he couldn't. Why hadn't Giulia warned him? A party with Pamina and her family... it was too much. They weren't supposed to be laying down roots.

"I..." he faltered.

The crestfallen look she gave him felt like a punch in the gut. He hated himself for disappointing her, but it was for the better. For both of them.

"Well, I guess I should start on the pies," Pamina said softly, eyes darting away.

Lorenzo watched as she carried the basket to the counter. He followed, feeling a mix of emotions. Taking a deep breath, he tried to calm himself. The last thing he needed was to have a panic attack in front of her.

"May I help you?" the question slipped out of him.

Pamina glanced up and smiled. "Of course. I'd like that."

Trying his best not to react to her nearness, Lorenzo turned to grab two mugs from the cupboard. He took the carafe and poured them each some caffé while Pamina gathered the rest of the supplies. The smell of the fresh brew filled his lungs, but it wasn't strong enough to completely mask the subtle honey scent of Pamina's soap.

Lorenzo stirred in the sugar, his pulse quickening. Warmth radiated from the beautiful witch, and it was all he could do to keep his distance. A hard task given the small workspace and his large stature.

"Excuse me," Pamina said, reaching for the cupboard behind him.

Lorenzo shifted himself, trying to get out of her way. Pamina stood tip-toed beside him, and her nearness drove him to distraction.

"Here. Let me," he said gruffly, setting his mug down and retrieving the little pie dishes she wanted.

His arm briefly brushed hers and though they were both wearing long-sleeves, the touch sent a rush of heat across his skin.

A low hiss escaped him. Pamina's eyes widened.

"Thank you," she said with a hurt look.

Did she mistake his desire for disgust? Distress filled Lorenzo at the thought. Surely, she knew how beautiful she was.

"Are you ready?" Pamina asked, snapping him to attention.

Lorenzo gave her a curt nod.

"How about if you mix all the ingredients and I'll roll the dough and prepare it."

He nodded at her, forcing himself to pay attention to her words and not her lips. Her pink, full lips.

She walked away to get the dough from the cooler. Lorenzo released his breath and turned his attention to the ingredients before him. Mixing them was the easier task, but he didn't mind. Anything to get his mind off Pamina.

"It looks like we'll need another cooling stone to put in the cooler soon. Or perhaps my sister could come and re-enchant the one in there now," Pamina said as she reappeared with the container.

"I'll buy another one when Giulia comes in."

Pamina set down the container and glanced at him. Though the counter was long, they would be working side by side. So close together.

Lorenzo swallowed hard and returned his focus to the pie. He measured the spices and dumped them into the large mixing bowl, breathing in their tantalizing aroma. Cinnamon, ginger, nutmeg, and cloves. Next, he measured the sugar, salt, and flour and stirred them in.

As he whisked the eggs to add, he noticed Pamina watching him with a smile.

She turned back to rolling out the dough. "You look so happy and peaceful when you're working."

Lorenzo pondered her words as he stirred in the eggs and added the milk and cream. He did enjoy working in the kitchen. For a moment, he'd forgotten it was the old man's kitchen.

The puree made a loud 'plop' as he poured it into the large bowl. The strong smell of pumpkin filled the kitchen along with the spices. A fire crackled and wagon wheels sounded from outside. The only sound in the silence besides his racing heart.

He finished mixing all the ingredients and watched as Pamina carefully laid out the rolled-out pie dough in each of the little dishes. She flicked a hand over them, and the cracks disappeared, leaving smooth bottoms and fancy swirling crust.

"No wonder all your pies turn out so perfectly," Lorenzo muttered.

Pamina's eyes met his, an uncertain look on her face.

"I meant no offense. Your baking magic... is actually quite impressive," he said as he poured his mixture into each of the pie dishes.

She smiled at him, making his heart stutter.

He stepped aside as she opened the oven behind them. Heat rushed out. Lorenzo handed her the pies, one at a time, to slide in.

Each time, their hands touched, and a thrill ran up his back. The kitchen was growing too warm, and it wasn't because of the oven.

Closing the door, Pamina turned to him and took a ragged breath.

Before he could stop himself, Lorenzo inched toward her. Her eyes widened and her mouth parted.

Waiting to see if she'd back away or come closer, he paused

and tried to steady his heart. His pulse quickened. He wanted to kiss her. He wanted to kiss her with every fiber of his being, but he wouldn't force himself on her. No.

If she wanted this, as he desperately hoped she did, she would meet him in the middle.

Her eyes implored him and just as he thought she was going to turn away, she didn't.

She took a step toward him. Their bodies were nearly touching.

His breath hitched.

"Lorenzo?" she said, eyes darting to his mouth.

A low groan escaped him at hearing his name on her lips. Desire flared in her brown eyes, and he was lost. There was no stopping what came next.

In one final step, he bent down and kissed her. Her lips were soft against his and the taste of sugar filled his mouth. It was the taste of *her*. Sugary sweet. Everything he was not, and he wanted—needed—more of it.

She returned his kiss, mouth moving against his. Eagerly. Hungrily. Heat raced along his skin. He pulled her toward him, arms encircling her waist. Their bodies pressed together. Soft against hard.

Pamina moaned and it was the most intoxicating, arousing sound he'd ever heard. His fingers dug deeper into her hips as he moved her away from the stove. He trailed kisses down her neck, breathing in her sweet honey smell.

They were at the door now, heading for the back room. The kitchen and then the bedroom. *His* bedroom.

That thought sent a cold dose of reality through him. What was he doing? He'd gone too far. This was too much.

He leapt away from Pamina, panting.

Surprise flashed on her face. Her curls had been shaken loose from her wrap, her face flushed, and her lips swollen.

Lorenzo bit back a groan and turned away from her. From those big brown eyes that asked for something he could never give. Their ragged breathing filled the room.

"I'm sorry. This was... a mistake," Lorenzo said with a hiss.

Pamina's sharp intake of breath made him wince.

"A mistake? I... don't understand. Don't regret your actions on my part. I wanted this too."

Her words speared him with longing and regret. Pamina wanted him and he wanted her, but he knew a dalliance with her wouldn't be enough. If he let himself give in, he'd want more. He'd want it all. A home. A family. A life with her.

But she'd never leave Zamerra or her family, and he could never make a home there.

"Lor—"

He whipped back to her and schooled his features. "Please forgive me, Signorina. I've acted reproachfully and I swear it will never happen again. I think it best if you take the day off."

Her eyes turned watery. "What? No. Why are you doing this?"

She deserved the truth at least.

Steeling himself, he continued. "Because it is what's best. Obviously, I can't deny my attraction, but I'm afraid that's all it is. It was never my plan to stay here. I'm here to help Giulia get the bakery running, and then I'll be leaving. And I don't plan to return."

Pamina's eyes narrowed. "You're leaving? Why? Because of me?"

Lorenzo shook his head. "No. You're the only reason, besides my sister, I've stayed this long. But I can't live here. I can't run this bakery."

Pamina nodded and dropped her gaze. "I see. I'm not reason enough for you to stay."

With that, she turned away and grabbed her coat off the

rack. Lorenzo watched her rush out the door, coat in hand, and he felt something inside him crack. Only this time, it wasn't his heart warming. No. It was breaking.

He hadn't known that was still possible.

"Pamina? What's wrong?"

He heard Giulia's voice outside. Stepping closer to the front window, he watched as Pamina waved his sister away and hurried down the street.

Giulia threw open the door, fire in her eyes. "What have you done?"

He sighed. The door slammed shut behind her, echoing loudly in the silence.

"I kissed her."

Her eyes widened. She frowned. "Why was she so upset? Did she not... I thought..."

"I kissed her and then I told her it was a mistake. Told her it could never be."

Giulia swore and pointed a finger at him. "You need to go after her and fix this, Lor. Now! You can't let her get away."

Lorenzo shook his head. "No, Giulia. This is what's best. Please. I—"

Giulia stamped her foot. "No! Tell me you don't love her, Lor. Look me in the eyes and tell me."

He met her furious glare. "I don't love her, Giulia."

His sister shut her eyes, looking as if he'd hurt her. "You're lying to yourself then, brother. Don't run away from your feelings like this. Don't be like..." the words died on her lips.

But Lorenzo knew who she meant.

He staggered back as if she'd slapped him. He wished she had. That wouldn't have hurt as badly.

Instant remorse flashed on her face. "Lor, I didn't mean..."

She reached a hand out to him, but he turned away. His heart hammered in his chest, her words replaying in his head.

He wasn't their father. He wasn't.

Grabbing his coat from the rack, he threw it on and fled out the door. He needed to get away and clear his mind, steady his breathing.

What had he done?

Chapter 15

Sweet Sixteen

Pamina

The next days blurred together as Pamina and Giulia worked to prepare everything for the festival. Thankfully, Lorenzo was never present, but Pamina couldn't get him off her mind. The memory of their kiss flashed before her, bringing back all the emotions.

It was never my plan to stay here. His words played on repeat in her mind.

It had never been her plan to fall for the half-goblin, but she had. Fallen hard.

Much to her relief, Giulia didn't press her for information, but the pitying look she gave her made Pamina suspect her brother had told her everything.

She couldn't tell her sisters. Not after Liliana warned her about *embarrassing* the family. Though Mama didn't ask, there was a knowing look in her eye and more frequent hugs. She was probably waiting for Pamina to open up and share, but Pamina just wanted to forget.

The mornings were packed with work at the bakery and the

evenings were filled with helping Mama and her sisters with the garden and their own festival preparations.

Even with her magical caffè, Pamina could hardly stay awake most nights. As soon as her head hit her pillow, she fell asleep, dreaming of a certain dark-eyed man. When she woke, the pain was all too fresh.

"Pamina, you're still in bed, *amore*? Are you feeling unwell?" Mama's voice startled her from her thoughts.

Pamina sat up and sighed. "I'm fine, Mama. Just moving slowly today."

Mama walked into the room and sat down on the end of her bed. Her dark eyes searched Pamina's. "This day off will be good for you. You've been overworking yourself."

"Is Serafina up already?"

Her mother shook her head. "No. But I'm sure she will be soon. Did you know that today is her birthday?" Mama asked with a gleam in her eyes.

Pamina tried to muster a smile at her mother's joke. Serafina had been giving them a daily countdown to her birthday and driving them all crazy with her roller coaster of emotions.

"I love you and I'm here for you, Pamina. You know you can always tell me anything." Mama kissed her forehead and brushed her hair back.

"I know. Thank you, Mama."

After another kiss, Mama turned to leave.

"Hello! Why is everyone still in bed? Get up! There's much to do!" Serafina's shrill voice echoed from down the hall.

Mama paused in the doorway and smiled at Pamina. "The birthday queen awakens."

* * *

Their home had never been so clean. Much to everyone's amusement, the enchanted villa pitched in and handled most of the work, sweeping the floors, washing the walls, dusting all the furniture and knick-knacks. Alessia and Liliana had come to help as well along with the men, Lucia, and little Franny.

Serafina, taking her role as birthday 'queen' very seriously, directed everyone as they put up decorations. Fiorella's green leaf garland was covered with bright, colorful, and fragrant flowers. Liliana brought her vanilla-scented candles and Pamina helped Mama set up a large table in their foyer, the only space large enough to host everyone.

"Oh, Pamina! That cannoli cake looks amazing. You'll have to teach me that recipe." Giulia's voice startled Pamina.

She turned to find the front door open and her friend standing there, wearing a purple velvet coat that looked much too fancy for a simple birthday party.

Giulia turned to wave to the driver as he stared curiously at the villa. The door slammed shut, making Giulia jump.

Her eyes widened. "What was that?"

Pamina smiled and took the gift from her friend. "Our villa is enchanted."

Giulia glanced around, eyes lighting up. "Really? Oh, how marvelous! I've never been in an enchanted villa before."

The young woman's brightness was infectious. It was almost enough to make Pamina forget the fact that Lorenzo hadn't come. Though he hadn't given her a definite answer, she'd secretly been hoping he would come.

Looping her arm in Pamina's Giulia walked over to greet Signora Silveri and the others. Pamina hung her friend's coat up and forced a smile. This was Serafina's special day, and she wouldn't ruin it with thoughts of Lorenzo.

Salvatore, Adriano, and Angelo arrived next, and the villa grew even more crowded. At least Serafina hadn't insisted on letting all their cats and Gio inside as well. Only Lucia got the privilege of attending the party, which didn't seem to impress her much. She curled herself up on the couch by the fire, away from the people and noise.

Pamina wished she could join her, but that would be rude. So, she finished laying out all the delicious food—all vegetarian or sweets for Serafina—and took part in the festivities. Serafina and Fiorella led the group through various games while Mama played them music from the piano.

It was nearly time to eat when a knock sounded at the door.

"Who could that be?" Serafina asked with a frown. She tore off the blindfold she'd had on and started walking to the front door.

"I'll get it! You keep playing, Fina," Pamina said, hurrying over to cut her off.

Her heart leapt into her throat. Was it Lorenzo? Had he changed his mind?

Excitement swept over her. She smoothed down her dress and went to open the door.

"Signor Rivaldi?" Pamina couldn't hide the surprise in her voice.

The tailor's son stood before her, looking handsome in his dark pants and fitted jacket. He removed his hat and grinned at her.

"Pamina, who is it?" Serafina asked, coming up behind her.

Everyone else had followed, much to Pamina's embarrassment. What was Stefano doing there?

"Happy birthday, Signorina!" Stefano said as he held out a wrapped gift to Fiorella.

Fiorella gaped at him.

Serafina folded her arms across her chest and huffed. "It's *my* birthday. And I didn't invite you."

"Fina!" Alessia scolded her.

She stepped forward and waved Stefano forward. "Welcome, Signor Rivaldi. We didn't know you'd be coming. What a lovely surprise!"

Serafina opened her mouth to protest, but Mama snatched her back and whispered something to her.

Everyone looked from Pamina to Stefano. Pamina's stomach rolled. She glanced at the empty doorway before Dante closed it. He gave her a curious look, eyebrow arched, but she had nothing to say.

She thought it would be Lorenzo. She wanted it to be him.

"You're just in time to feast with us, Signor," Mama said warmly.

"But we didn't put a place out for him," Fiorella said aloud.

Mama laughed off her sister's words and chattered on. Pamina was thankful she wasn't expected to speak yet.

Liliana sidled up to her with a glare. "What is he doing here, Pamina? What were you thinking by inviting him here? What if he sees..." She fell silent as Giulia approached.

The young woman gave Pamina a sheepish look. "I'm afraid, it's my fault he's here. I mentioned the party when I was in the tailor's shop. But I never imagined he'd show up. Uninvited. How... bold." She turned to look at the man in question.

Liliana snorted. "Bold alright. And rude. And—"

Dante cut her off with a kiss that made Pamina blush. Giulia's eyebrows shot to her forehead.

Alessia stormed over and gave Liliana and Dante a scalding look. "Enough of that, you two. Listen, I need you all to help manage Fiorella and Serafina while the guests are here." Her eyes darted to Giulia.

Pamina nodded to Alessia, well aware of the predicament they were in. No one, but their neighbors came to their villa and even they weren't privy to the younger girl's magic.

"Come on, everyone. We can't let the food get too cold!" Mama's voice echoed through the foyer.

They took their seats, an awkward tension in the air. A place had been set for Stefano beside Pamina. She put on her best smile and turned to him. Lorenzo hadn't come, and though Stefano hadn't been invited, at least he was showing an effort. Maybe she'd been wrong about him.

He returned her smile, his sea-green eyes dipping to her chest.

"You're looking lovely today, Signorina," he murmured, gaze still glued to her dress.

Pamina cleared her throat. "Thank you."

He tore his eyes away and glanced down the table. "Where is your goblin friend?"

Everyone fell silent. Giulia, on Pamina's other side, stiffened.

She leaned past Pamina to peer at Stefano. "I'm right here," she said flatly.

Stefano frowned at her. "No, I mean your brother. He wasn't invited?"

Annoyance flickered on Giulia's face, but before she could answer, Pamina spoke up. "He was, but he couldn't make it,"

Stefano tutted. "What a shame."

Pamina's brow furrowed. Is that why Stefano had come? Was this just some kind of competition for him?

"I'd rather he had come than you, Signor. At least he knows when to keep his mouth shut," Serafina said from the opposite end of the table.

Mama and Alessia shot her a glare.

Stefano's mouth dropped open, face flushing with anger. Serafina gave him a savage smile and took a sip of her wine.

A mixture of amused delight and shocked horror rippled

through the group. Pamina shook her head, face warming. This party was going to be a disaster.

As if on cue, two high-pitched squeals sounded from the kitchen. Bruno and Franny came running into the foyer, hand in hand, deciding this was the proper time to make their appearance. The little elves climbed into Massimo's lap and jumped onto the table before the fae could grab them.

"House elves! I knew it!" Angelo shouted.

Salvatore yelped as the pair jumped over his plate, nearly knocking his glass over. Adriano's wineglass, they did knock, sending the red liquid over the edge and into Fiorella's lap.

"My dress!" She cried.

"Bruno! Franny! Stop it. Stop it this instance!" Alessia yelled, rising to her feet. Massimo echoed her in Elvish.

Shouts rang out, but the elves didn't stop. They raced down the table, heading straight for the cannoli cake at the end and leaving chaos in their wake.

Pamina threw a hand over her mouth. *Santo Cielo.* The only thing that would make it worse was if...

A chorus of meows and Gio's bark sounded from the hall.

"Serafina! What have you done?" Mama demanded as all the outdoor cats and Gio poured into the foyer.

But Serafina wasn't paying attention. The elves had made it to her and their prize. She held a hand up to them in warning.

"Don't you dare," she said.

Pamina sucked in a breath. "No! Don—"

It was too late. Bruno and Franny launched themselves at the cake, toppling the top layer right off and onto the floor. The cats and Gio went wild, fighting over the droppings.

Everyone was shouting. Angelo had burst into laughter, earning him a glare from Serafina and a smack from his brother. Fiorella was crying over her dress and Giulia's eyebrows had shot so far up her forehead, they were practically part of her hairline now.

Pamina turned to Stefano. The wide-eyed look of horror on his face was just as she expected.

She gave him a weak smile. "Would you like me to walk you out, Signor?"

He blinked at her and glanced back at the elves, who were now covered in cake. Bruno let out an epic belch and dodged Alessia's grasp. Franny started throwing cake at the cats, giggling with glee as the poor animals yowled.

Stefano shot out of his chair and nodded to Pamina. "Yes. I... I have to go."

Pamina followed him to the front door and handed him his coat.

He took it quickly and stepped outside. Cold air swirled in as the door opened and the juniper tree in the front yard shook violently, bending toward the villa.

Pamina bit back a groan. Fiorella's magic. Not wanting Stefano to notice anything was amiss, she followed him outside quickly.

His horse whinnied, trying to break free from the tree he'd tethered it to. The poor beast was probably terrified.

Stefano stroked its side, trying to soothe it. Pamina folded her arms across herself, shivering in the cold.

The trees stopped suddenly, and the horse settled. Stefano turned around, surprised to see her there.

Pamina walked up to him and sighed. "I'm sorry, Signor. Thank you for coming. I hope this incident hasn't tarnished your opinion of my family."

Stefano grunted. "Your family is as uncouth and deplorable as everyone says."

Anger zipped through Pamina's veins. "I beg your pardon?"

He gave her a contemptuous smile. "However, I don't

include you in that estimation, *bella*. You are much better than your family. You must know how I feel about you."

Pamina's mouth dropped open. "How you feel about me?"

Stefano took her by the hands and nodded. "Of course. Let me show you."

Before she could register what he'd said, his mouth was on hers. Pamina was too stunned to react. When she tried to move away, his hands gripped her face, holding her in place.

This was nothing like the kiss Lorenzo had given her. This was not a kiss of love or even passion. It was dominance and possession.

She yanked at his hands, trying to break the kiss. He withdrew and frowned at her, a look of irritation on his face.

Fury and disgust rolled through her. She was too angry to speak.

"Forgive me, Signorina. I only wanted to show you how I felt. Perhaps I got too carried away." Stefano gave her a satisfied smile and turned to his horse.

"Well, it won't happen again. Will it, Signor?" Pamina asked, making it clear it wasn't a true question.

Stefano scowled but said nothing. He untethered his horse and mounted it, bareback, waving at Pamina as he rode off.

She watched him go, letting the cold wind cool her anger. It was clear, her sister had been right about Stefano, and shame filled her at the thought of telling her family what had happened. What if Stefano told everyone? What would Lorenzo do if he found out?

A scoff escaped her. What would he do? He would do nothing. He'd made it clear he didn't want her.

Chapter 16

The Letter

Lorenzo

The Harvest Festival was only a few days away and Lorenzo was ready to leave the town and everything behind. Though he'd made up with Giulia there was still a tension between them. One he hoped would go away before it was time for him to go. At least she had stopped pestering him about Pamina.

After hearing that Stefano had come to call on the beautiful witch, he'd told himself he had made the right choice in letting her go. Now she was free to pursue a courtship with the tailor's son.

It was better he hadn't gone to the party, though with Giulia's retelling, it sounded like it had been a party he would have thoroughly enjoyed. If only the house elves had spilled wine on Pamina's admirer and thrown cake at him.

"Lor, you're smiling. I haven't seen that in a while. Are you thinking about Pamina?" Giulia asked softly, looking up from the mail she had spread across the table.

Lorenzo frowned and glanced around the dining room. Thankfully the innkeeper and his family weren't around to hear his sister's loud mouth. And they were the only guests staying there.

"What is that?" he asked.

"A letter. What does it look like?" his sister retorted.

Lorenzo scowled. "Yes, but who is it from? Gemma?"

Giulia waved the letter at him. "Don't try and change the subject."

She opened it and started reading, still scolding him. "You can't keep ignoring her, Lor. This is getting out of hand, really. Don't you—" She stopped suddenly, her eyes still on the letter.

"What is it? What's wrong? Giulia?"

Lorenzo held his breath, hoping it wasn't what he'd feared.

It couldn't be.

Giulia's eyes snapped to his. "It's from Riccardo."

Lorenzo tried to make his face look neutral. "How did he know to send it here? I thought he was still overseas."

His sister stared at him, a desperate look in her eyes. She waved the letter at Lorenzo. "Tell me this isn't true, Lor. Tell me you had no part in this."

Lorenzo's insides turned to ice. So, the man had returned from his trip and found out what they'd done. He knew it would be a matter of time before they would hear from him. When he had originally planned the scheme, he'd been counting on him and Giulia being far in the Regno Unito and unreachable.

"You knew about this, didn't you?" Giulia's voice had gone hoarse.

Lorenzo couldn't stand the look of betrayal on her face. He looked away.

Giulia gave a harsh laugh. "No. This *was* you. It was your idea, wasn't it? To have his parents fake that letter? To make it seem like he'd fled after he sent it?"

Her voice cracked. "How could you?"

"Giulia, I had to. You would have married him!"

Giulia slammed the letter down on the table, making the silverware rattle. "Yes! Yes, I would have married him. You had no right!"

"Please. Lower your—"

"No! I will not lower my voice, Lor. How could you?" Giulia's voice rang in the dining room.

Lorenzo flinched at the rawness of her voice. He'd gone too far. He knew he'd gone too far when he did it, but couldn't she see he'd done it out of love?

"I know what his family thinks of me. Thinks of us. I accepted that, Lor. I knew what I was getting myself into. You had no right to do this."

"I couldn't see you end up like Mother." He choked out the words.

Giulia took a deep breath. "Mother loved our father, Lor. Even for all his faults. She could have remarried. There were offers, and I know you remember that. She had us and she had Father when he came, and it was enough for her."

His sister shook her head and fell silent. "I don't know why Father didn't stay, Lor and we may never know, but Riccardo is not him. I am not Mother."

Lorenzo bit back the argument on his tongue. It would only drive his sister away, and he'd already done a superb job at that.

Giulia met his gaze. "I'm leaving. I'll stay for the festival, but then I'm gone. I love you, Lor, but you've wounded me so deeply. I'm marrying Riccardo, and if you can't accept that..." she sniffed, blinking back tears, "then I guess this will be goodbye."

Her words sliced through him. Giulia was leaving. Just like their father. Just like Niccola. The image his broken heart dredged up wasn't of his ex-fiancée, but a brown-eyed witch instead.

"I'm sorry," Lorenzo said softly as his sister gathered her things.

She looked at him through teary eyes and nodded. "I know you are. I... I just need some time. I don't think I can come to the bakery tomorrow."

With that she left the dining room, leaving Lorenzo alone. He stared down at his hands and took a ragged breath. Was he destined to end up alone just like his father?

It seemed that way and perhaps that's what he deserved.

With time running out, Lorenzo couldn't leave Pamina to finish all the work alone. So, with much reluctance, he made his way to the bakery. Hopefully, her caffé could help the bruised feeling he had. He'd given Giulia the space she'd requested, still feeling guilty and ashamed of what he'd done. Just because he was destined to live a lonely miserable life, didn't mean she was.

He was glad Riccardo had sent that letter even If it meant exposing his lie. It felt better to have it off his chest. Hopefully, in time he could make it up to his sister.

"Oh. Good morning. Where's Giulia?" Pamina's gentle voice made him jump.

Lorenzo rose, the fire crackling behind him. "Good morning. Giulia won't be in today, but I'm here to help. Unless you'd rather I leave you to it?"

Pamina hung up her coat, her back to him. "The help would be appreciated, but you don't have to."

Her voice was barely above a whisper, hurt lacing each word. Lorenzo searched his mind for something to say. Something to put her at ease. He hated seeing her hurt and he hated himself for being the one who had hurt her.

"Pamina, I enjoy working with you. I never meant to hurt you. It seems I'm even more of a toad than I realized."

Her brow furrowed at him. "I never called you a toad."

His lips quirked into a smile. Even after he'd hurt her, she still grew offended on his behalf.

"No, but you should. I've upset you and now my sister."

Pamina's eyes widened. "You upset Giulia? How?"

Lorenzo blew out a loud breath and motioned for her to carry the carafe to the counter. "It's a long story."

"We have a long day ahead of us. But if you don't want to tell me, I understand."

He watched as she walked past and busied herself in the kitchen. What would it hurt to tell her the whole story? Giulia would tell her eventually before she left. And once his sister left, there would definitely be no more reason for him to stay.

After a giant mug of caffé and a few pumpkin muffins, he felt much better. Pamina sipped from her own mug and waited patiently as he spilled everything to her.

Embarrassingly enough, he couldn't help but choke up when he got to the end, where Giulia had told him she was leaving. Of course, Pamina wasn't one to judge.

She listened to him, a look of sympathy on her face.

"And so, that's everything. Giulia will be gone after the festival and once I've sold and packed up, I'll be gone too."

Pamina frowned. "Where will you go?"

Lorenzo shrugged miserably. "Maybe back to the city."

They fell quiet.

"Giulia knows you love her. You shouldn't have done what you did, but I think in time, she'll be able to forgive you."

He scoffed. "I don't deserve her forgiveness."

"Of course, you do." Her eyes searched his. "Sometimes, forgiveness is more for us than the other person anyway."

"What do you mean?"

She cocked her head at him and continued. "My father left too. When I was a baby. I don't even remember him, but it still

147

hurt. It hurt for a long time wondering who he was, what he was doing. If he ever thought about me."

A sad smile spread on her face, nearly ripping him in two.

"I was angry too. But when I got older, I realized holding onto that anger was only hurting me. I forgave him, not because he deserved it, but because I needed to, so I could move past it."

"You sound like my mother and Giulia."

Pamina shrugged. "They only want your happiness."

Lorenzo looked down into his near-empty mug, a lump growing in his throat. "Are you happy, Pamina?"

His gaze flickered to her. Surprise flashed on her face. She pursed her lips and glanced around at the bakery.

"Yes. I think so. Sometimes, I wonder what it would have been like to grow up somewhere else. Where magic was more accepted and my family wasn't the frequent target for gossip, but I love Zamerra."

"Even if it doesn't love you?" Lorenzo asked softly.

She smiled. "My family loves me and my friends. I don't need everyone's approval."

"What about Stefano?" Lorenzo couldn't help but ask.

Her smile vanished. A strange look crossed her face, making Lorenzo frown.

Shaking off the look, she turned to him. "I don't need his approval either."

He wasn't sure how to read her words and didn't want to spend what few days they had left talking about Stefano.

"Thank you for listening. And sharing," he said instead.

Pamina laid a hand on top of his, warmth spreading from the contact.

His eyes met hers. Something stirred inside him at her frank, open stare. Here was a woman, who'd gone through heartache and been labeled an outcast too, but instead of choosing bitterness, as he had, she'd chosen kindness.

The town didn't deserve her. *He* didn't deserve her.

"I wish I could kiss you again." The words slipped from his mouth.

Pamina flushed. "Why can't you?"

He sucked in a breath at her invitation. There was nothing he'd like more than to taste her sweet lips again.

"Pamina, I'm still leaving. After the festival."

She moved toward him, her scent invading his senses. A sad smile spread on her face. "Yes. I know. You keep telling me. But I wish you'd stay."

With that, she tilted her face up to meet his. Lorenzo bent toward her, memorizing every detail. Her closed eyes, rosy cheeks, and quivering lips.

Then he kissed her. His hands snaked around her waist, pulling her taut against him. Her hands splayed his chest, warmth blossoming through his body. He took her bottom lip gently between his teeth, and the moan it elicited from her made him mad with desire.

She was sweet and warm. He kissed her fervently, desperate for the moment to stretch as long as possible. Pamina Silveri was unlike any woman he'd ever known or would ever know again. He knew in that moment, she'd claimed his heart, and he hadn't even realized he still had one.

Pulling away from him, she gasped for breath. "As enjoyable as that is... we should probably get started on the cupcakes."

Her words echoed somewhere in Lorenzo's mind. It took all his willpower to shift his focus from her to baking. What had started as a simple business arrangement had quickly and surprisingly become something much more.

Chapter 17

The Insult

Pamina

"I suppose my brother told you what he did?" Giulia's question interrupted Pamina's thoughts.

She banished the memory of Lorenzo's kiss and turned to her friend.

"Yes, he did. He's very sorry too."

Giulia nodded. "I know. It was a terrible thing. Even if he meant it out of love."

The echo of their boots against the cobblestone filled the silence. It was the day before the Harvest Festival and though Lorenzo hadn't kissed her again, he'd been present, helping her in the bakery. Pamina couldn't help but smile as her mind drifted to their time together.

She'd never met a man as talented in the kitchen as Lorenzo. Apart from Signor Covelli, which she knew not to bring up to Lorenzo. It pained her that he still carried his anger and hurt. All the pies in the world wouldn't be enough to completely heal him.

He needed to choose it for himself. Even if he still left

Zamerra and left her behind, she hoped he would be able to move on from the past. He deserved to let himself be happy.

"Pamina? Did you hear me?" Giulia asked, giving her a curious look.

"Oh, sorry. I got distracted. What were you saying?"

Giulia's eyes narrowed at her in thought before she continued. "I was saying you should come visit me in the city. You and your sisters. Your mother too, of course." She lowered her voice and glanced around the street. "Oh, and the little elves too."

Pamina smiled at her friend. "That would be nice. Thank you. And you have to come back to Zamerra too. At least to check on the bakery."

Giulia stopped abruptly and threw her arms around Pamina. "It's yours, you know."

She let go of Pamina and gave her a guilty look. "Sorry. Lorenzo wanted to tell you, but ooh, I just can't keep it secret any longer."

Pamina gaped at her. Was she saying what she thought she was?

"The bakery, Pamina. It's yours, if you want it. Lorenzo and I both agreed you should have it."

"Me? Oh, Giulia. I... I don't know what to say. I appreciate you thinking of me, but I can't... I don't have the money... well, I guess I could talk to Massimo. He did mention something..."

Giulia's eyes gleamed with delight. "Don't worry about the money. It will all work itself out."

Pamina thanked her again and followed as she continued walking. They were giving her the bakery. A part of her was thrilled, but there was another part of her that felt disappointed.

Running a bakery seemed like a dream come true, but what would it be like working there without Lorenzo?

Her throat turned dry.

"Ahh. Look! They still have some wreaths left," Giulia said pointing across the street to the general store.

With the pastries and treats ready for the festival, they had spent the day decorating and preparing the shop for its first customers.

Just as her friend started to head that way, Pamina spotted Stefano and his friends walking toward them.

Not wanting to face him, she grabbed Giulia's arm and pulled her behind one of the shops.

Giulia turned to her with a frown. Pamina held a finger up to her lip in warning. Stefano and the others grew closer. Giulia peeked around the building before Pamina yanked her back. She didn't want the men to see them.

"Shut up, Loui, you're just jealous." Stefano's voice rang loud and clear.

His friend snorted. "Me? Jealous? Not a chance. No offense, Stefano, but I don't see what you see in that girl. If she's this big now, can you imagine how much bigger she'll be after children? Do you really want to be stuck with a fat heifer?"

Heat flooded Pamina's face. Giulia gasped beside her. A look of hot rage flashed across her features. She looked as if she were about to stomp over to them, but Pamina grabbed her by the wrist and shook her head.

Surely, Stefano would defend her? He wouldn't let his friend talk like that, would he? He was awful, but not *that* awful.

Stefano laughed. A short laugh that made Pamina's stomach churn.

"Who said anything about marrying? I don't want to wed the heifer. I just want to—"

Giulia ripped herself from Pamina's hold and burst around the building. Shoving down her embarrassment and hurt, Pamina followed her.

The group gave an alarmed cry as Giulia advanced on them. "How dare you speak like that! You disgusting swine."

Pamina's eyes bulged. "Giulia!"

Though she appreciated her friend's support, she didn't like the crowd she was drawing. People had stepped out of their stores to watch the altercation.

One of the young men sneered. "It was a private conversation, you toad."

Pamina gasped. Anger rolled through her at his insult.

Giulia only laughed. "As if I haven't heard *that* one."

Pamina tugged at her arm, trying to pull her away. "Come on!"

But Giulia wouldn't be swayed. She stood her ground, glaring at the men. People were walking over now. Pamina looked up to see Lorenzo striding over, a murderous look on his face.

Santo Cielo.

She needed to get Giulia away before things got out of hand.

"What's going on?" Lorenzo bellowed, making it to them in only a few steps.

Stefano's eyes narrowed on him. "Your sister has lost her mind. Must be that goblin blood."

"That's right. Goblins are prone to hysterics and violence. You can't fault her if it's in her nature," another man piped in.

Pamina's head snapped toward him. "That's not true at all, you vile man!"

Lorenzo stepped between them, towering over the group. "Not another word about my sister, or I'll show you how *violent* goblins can be."

His voice was like steel. Pamina moved to see what was happening.

Stefano glanced at Pamina. "You really should be more

careful with the company you keep, Signorina. As sweet as your kisses may be, you can hardly expect me to allow such poor judgment on your part."

Giulia gasped beside her. Other gasps echoed behind them. Lorenzo stiffened and glanced back at her, a look of hurt on his face.

"No. I..." Pamina faltered.

Heat spread up her back at everyone's stares. The other's shocked looks she could manage, but the betrayed look Lorenzo gave her cut through her like a knife.

"Come on. We have work to finish," Lorenzo finally said, motioning Giulia and Pamina away.

Stefano and his friends snickered, shouting insults to Lorenzo's back as they left.

"Don't listen to those *asesinos,* Signor," a man spoke up, throwing a disgusted look at Stefano.

Another woman nodded. "They shouldn't speak such awful things."

Lorenzo nodded in acknowledgment to their supporters before leading them past. Wreath, forgotten, they returned to the bakery. Everyone was quiet.

"Do either of you care to tell me what that was about?" Lorenzo asked once they'd gathered at the little back table.

Giulia glanced at Pamina.

Pamina's face warmed. She didn't want to tell Lorenzo what they'd heard. She didn't want to tell him about Stefano's kiss either, but worried he was thinking the worst.

What if he actually believed she preferred that oaf?

"No? No one is going to tell me?" Lorenzo frowned at them.

Giulia sighed. "Let's just forget it altogether, Lor. We have to finish the decorations for tomorrow."

Pamina gave her a grateful smile, wondering if Giulia was thinking the same as her brother. She couldn't bear the thought of them thinking she had kissed Stefano willingly, but she didn't know how to tell them what had happened.

Lorenzo studied her before finally turning away.

"Those donkey asses made me forget the wreath," Giulia muttered, frowning.

"We could go to my villa. Fiorella would be thrilled to make one for you," Pamina offered.

Giulia clapped her hands together. "Oh, that would be perfect!"

Pamina turned to Lorenzo. "You can come too if you like."

A panicked look crossed his face. "No. No thank you. I'll stay here and finish things up. You two go."

His rejection stung. She couldn't help but feel as if she'd messed things up between them. Pushing the thought aside, she followed Giulia out back to rent a wagon.

While her friend chattered excitedly about wreaths and decorations, Pamina tried to listen. At least Giulia had put the whole thing behind her. Would Lorenzo be able to as well? She vowed to tell him the truth the next chance she got. It wouldn't be easy. It probably wouldn't change anything, but he deserved the truth. Even if he was still determined to leave.

Chapter 18

The Harvest Festival

Lorenzo

The day was gray and dreary. Not ideal for an outdoor Harvest Festival, but Lorenzo couldn't care less if it rained. In fact, a downpour that forced everyone to stay indoors sounded perfect to him. Then he wouldn't have to see anyone. Particularly Pamina.

Stefano's words replayed in his mind. *As sweet as your kisses may be.*

Whatever had followed after, Lorenzo hadn't heard. He hadn't even been aware of the insults the man had hurled at him until some of the townsfolk had spoken up for him.

The thought of Pamina kissing Stefano made his skin boil.

"Do you think it's even worth it to pull the cart outside? We... what did that poor napkin do to you?" Giulia's voice startled him out of his thoughts.

Lorenzo glanced down to see the crumpled cloth in his fist. He imagined it was Stefano's face. That made him smile.

"Lor? Are you listening to anything I'm saying?"

He dropped the napkin onto the counter and sighed. "When is Pamina arriving?"

Giulia shot him a flat look. "So, no then. You haven't been listening."

An irritated groan escaped him. "No, I don't think it's worth rolling that confounded cart outside. Why isn't Pamina here yet?"

Giulia snorted. "You're hopeless. I'm sure she's on her way. Relax, brother."

Relax. As if he could.

A flash of guilt crossed his sister's face. "I may have already accidentally told her about the bakery."

"What? Giulia, I thought we were going to tell her together. Now, who's hopeless?"

"Still you, Lor. There is so much I could say in regard to your vexing stubbornness, but I've already told you my opinion."

Lorenzo waved a dismissive hand. "Yes. Yes. More times than needed, thank you."

He sighed and looked down at the weak, bland caffé he'd brought from the inn. "She's obviously moved on so anything I say would be pointless."

Giulia's face hardened. "If this is about what that idiot said, you need to talk to Pamina. Ask her. Instead of taking your anger out on innocent cloths."

His sister was right, as usual, but Lorenzo didn't want to hear it. If Pamina hadn't kissed the man, why hadn't she just said so?

He rubbed his pounding head. "It's none of my business anyway. I—"

"Leaving. I know. We all know. You're making a mistake, Lor, but I won't stop you. You have to choose this for yourself."

"Hmm. Since when did you become so wise?"

Giulia threw him an annoyed look. "I've always been wise, Lor. You just never listen."

The sound of wagon wheels pulled up outside, drowning out whatever else his sister had to say. They both hurried to the front window to look out. The Silveris' wagon stopped in front of their store.

Lorenzo watched as Pamina and her sisters piled out. Their mother waved from her spot on the bench. Giulia waved back and glanced at Lorenzo.

"Aren't you going to go out and help with her horse?" She nudged him in the ribs.

Lorenzo, who'd been staring at Pamina, glanced at his sister and nodded. "Of course. I got distracted."

Giulia rolled her eyes.

Before he could get his coat on, Signor Lazzaro and Pamina's sister stepped out of their apothecary and went to help with the wagon.

"Oh, maybe she's having caffé with her family first," Giulia mused aloud as they watched the women embracing each other.

Lorenzo frowned. As heartwarming as it was to watch Pamina with her family, he had hoped to spend some time alone with her. Their time was so limited.

A knock interrupted his thoughts. Giulia opened the door and Pamina's youngest sister, Fiorella, popped her head in. "Hello! Would you like to join us for caffé and desserts?" the young girl asked, eyes darting across the bakery.

"We'd love to! Would you all like to come in here? We have plenty of space," Giulia offered.

"Oh, yes! Thank you. I'll tell the others."

Giulia exchanged a look with Lorenzo. "Careful, Lor. All this smiling and I hardly recognize you. You can't tell me you don't find Pamina and her family charming."

She sighed and shook her head. "I really wish you'd reconsider leaving."

Before Lorenzo could tell her, once again, that it was for the best, the door burst open. Pamina and her family filed in, boots loud against the wood floor.

Pamina and Alessia scolded them for not wiping their feet properly. Giulia waved it off and led everyone further into the shop.

Lorenzo moved to make room for the lively bunch. He waited as Pamina helped her sister out of her coat and hung it up. She turned to him, her eyes bright. Her brown curls were loose, a large red ribbon tied in a bow around her head. The red dress she wore hugged her curvy body, the gold buttons sparkling.

"You look beautiful," Lorenzo whispered, forgetting the audience they had.

Snickers and giggles echoed behind him, but he was too busy gawking at Pamina to notice or care.

She smiled at him shyly. "Thank you. It was a gift from Giulia. Your suit is dashing."

Giulia grabbed his arm and laughed. "I picked out the suit too. But I won't be going back to the tailor anytime soon."

Voices rang out around them, but Lorenzo tuned them out. This day would be one he'd cherish forever. In only three days' time, he and Giulia were leaving. She'd already booked them tickets and he'd settled everything with the count. Pamina would get the bakery. Giulia would get Riccardo and he would be left just as he started—with nothing.

Or you could stay. The thought jumped out at him.

It was frightening, how often it came to his mind. Even after the incident with Stefano, there was a part of him that envisioned himself staying. Living there. But it had nothing to do with the town and everything to do with the beautiful witch who stood before him.

She laughed at something his sister said, and it was the

loveliest sound in the world. Lorenzo joined, following her and Giulia to one of the tables.

Pamina's eyes met his as he sat down directly across from her. She smiled sadly at him, and it sent a spear of pain in his chest. Her words echoed in his ears.

I'm not reason enough for you to stay.

It wasn't true though. She was more than reason enough to stay, but how could he love her as she deserved to be loved when his heart was still filled with so much anger? He glanced around at the bakery, waiting for the bitterness he usually felt, but it didn't come. Somehow his father's bakery had come to feel like his own. His and Pamina's.

Memories of working side by side with Pamina flashed through his mind. But she kissed Stefano.

And she kissed you twice.

Tormented by his thoughts, Lorenzo took a sip of her magical brew and tried to quiet his mind. The warm liquid slid down his throat and settled his nerves. He was running out of time to figure everything out.

Chapter 19

The Dance

Pamina

L orenzo was quiet as they drank caffé, a stormy look on his face. Pamina's fingers itched to cast another contentment spell over the cookie in his hands. Her eyes dipped to his lips. Cookie crumbs gathered in the corner of his mouth, and she had the sudden urge to help him clean them off. With her mouth.

Heat flooded her at the thought. She turned away and tried to focus on the conversation drifting around them. Outside, people shouted and cheered, setting up their carts for the festival.

Mama had brought their own wares to sell. Giant pumpkins, winter squash, and dried herbs. Along with jars of pumpkin purée and Pamina's famous pies. Once the patrizio blew the horn, everyone would gather in the plaza to give thanks for a plentiful harvest. There would be music, food, dancing, and games.

Pamina's gaze drifted back to Lorenzo. With the busyness of the preparations, she hadn't found the time to talk to him about the other day. To explain herself. She certainly didn't want to tell him in front of everyone else.

"Well, I think I should get the cart ready to roll out," Lorenzo finally spoke, his eyes darting to Pamina.

"I can help you," Pamina said quickly. She rose to her feet to follow him.

"I'll be out shortly to help too. After I eat more of these delicious cookies," Giulia told them as she reached for another pumpkin-shaped treat.

"Do you need extra help?" Fiorella asked hopefully.

Mama laid a hand on top of hers. "We should go set up our crates and wagon, *amore*. Serafina?"

Pamina glanced at her sister. Since Angelo's departure, her sister hadn't been her usual talkative self. She was spending more time with her animals, and Pamina had found her staring forlornly at nothing. She'd tried on several occasions to talk to her, but Serafina wouldn't accept her comfort.

Not even the festival—which she normally loved—seemed able to cheer her up.

Pamina could hardly blame her. The thought of Lorenzo leaving and never returning filled her with such sorrow and dread.

"Fina?" Alessia prompted.

Trusting her older sisters to help with Serafina, Pamina turned away to catch up with Lorenzo. This was her chance to talk to him without everyone else around. She made her way to the back cooler and nearly ran into Lorenzo.

He swore, the tray of pies jostling in his hands. Thankfully, he had a strong hold and didn't let them drop.

"I... I wanted to talk to you. Do you mind?" Pamina asked.

Her heart drummed loudly in her ears. She rehearsed what she wanted to say, but standing there with Lorenzo, close enough to smell his woodsy scent, all sensible thought fled her.

"Yes?" he prompted, dark eyes searching her face.

Pamina took a deep breath and released it. "It's about Stefano."

Lorenzo's jaw clenched. His hands tightened on the tray.

Wanting to get everything off her chest, Pamina launched into the story, leaving no part of it out. When she finished, she forced herself to meet Lorenzo's eyes, nervous to see what she'd find there. Would he understand that she didn't have feelings for Stefano?

Lorenzo's face was hard. "Do you mean to tell me he *forced* himself on you?"

The iciness of his tone chilled Pamina. She reached a tentative hand out to him and touched his shoulder.

"I never cared for him, Lorenzo. You must believe me. He means nothing to me."

Lorenzo shut his eyes and let out a low growl. Pamina withdrew her hand, worried she'd upset him further.

He opened his eyes and stared at her. "I do. I do believe you, Pamina. What I can't believe is he had the audacity... the —" he fumed.

"He will pay for this."

Pamina's eyes widened at his murderous tone. "No, it's over. Please. He's not worth it, Lorenzo."

"But he—"

She held up a hand to cut him off. "I don't want to waste any more time on him. Please."

Lorenzo's jaw tightened, but he didn't argue. "If he—"

"He won't." Pamina shook her head.

"Are you two coming? Everyone is already setting up out there," Giulia called from the front room.

Pamina moved to let Lorenzo pass and grabbed another tray of cookies from the cooler. They took the pastries and goodies outside and started setting up the wooden, wheeled cart.

Pamina pulled her coat tighter as she watched Lorenzo turn on the little gas oven.

They'd sold the espresso machine to buy a portable one in time for the festival. Once it was ready, she helped Giulia load some of the mini pies into it. The warmth from the little oven blasted into the air before they closed it.

"I can stay here with the cart. Why don't you two go take a walk around? Maybe a dance or two!" Giulia said, shoving Lorenzo away from their stand.

He gave her an exasperated sigh. "Are you sure you don't want to explore? Do some shopping? There are a lot of carts and wagons out here."

Giulia glanced at the full plaza and bit her lip. "I'll explore later. When you get back. Now, go!"

Pamina took the arm Lorenzo offered her and waved goodbye to her friend. "I'm going to miss Giulia. And you. I'll miss you both."

Lorenzo glanced at her with a tortured look. "We'll both miss you as well. I..." He fell silent, shaking his head.

Disappointment ran through her. She wanted him to tell her he'd changed his mind. That he would stay. That he loved her.

Her heart stuttered at the unspoken wish. Did he love her? She loved him.

Pamina looked up at him, studying his profile. He stopped and returned her stare.

"What is it?" he asked, voice low and scratchy.

It sent a shiver up her spine.

"Pamina! They're about to start the music. Come on!" Fiorella ran by, interrupting them.

Serafina followed, though the resigned look on her face made Pamina suspect she was only going to keep an eye on Fiorella not to enjoy herself. The last time they'd all been at such a large town event had been Hallow's Eve, and Fiorella had been possessed by a wicked fae spirit.

Pamina shuddered at the awful memory. It had taken Dante and Liliana both to free poor Fiorella, and they'd smothered her magic even further to keep it from happening again. With Dante's magic gone now, Liliana was the only one who could perform such a spell. What would happen if Fiorella's full magic was released?

"Are you cold? Let's move closer to the fire." Lorenzo's voice broke through her thoughts.

"Oh, no. Sorry. I was just remembering something terrible."

Lorenzo frowned. "Do you wish to talk about it, or would you rather forget?"

Pamina shrugged in response. "It's not something we can talk about here anyway."

Seeing his confusion, she leaned closer into him and lowered her voice. "It's about my sister. Her magic. I would tell you, but then you would have more questions. Questions I can't answer here."

Lorenzo nodded in understanding and led her toward the center where a large bonfire had been started. The musicians were setting up and people milled about, sipping on spiced wine and hot cider. All the smells from the various carts clashed in the air.

"If I don't ask you to dance with me, I'll never hear the end of it from Giulia."

Pamina arched an eyebrow at him. "Is that an invitation then or just polite conversation?"

"I'm not known to be very polite."

"If you want to dance then ask me," she insisted.

His lips quirked into a smile. "Will you dance with me?"

Her heart leapt into her throat, her pulse quickening. "Yes. I would love to dance with you."

Lorenzo's eyes grew hooded. He walked her to an open space on the cobblestoned street and held her in his arms. The warmth of his touch filled her from her head to her toes. She breathed in his familiar scent, a longing spreading through her.

She tried not to think about his leaving. Or working in the bakery without him. Of never seeing him again.

A ballad started, the beautiful melancholy notes giving voice to her emotions. She pressed her head against his solid chest and closed her eyes, letting the music wash over her. He led her in a slow dance along the plaza. If people were whispering, she didn't care.

She could only hear the music. Feel his warmth radiating through her. It was a night she would never forget. Something she could hold onto when he left. When the world became mundane once more.

"Pamina." Lorenzo's low voice rang through her.

She opened her eyes and looked up at him.

"Look," he said glancing upward.

They stopped dancing. Everyone around them had stopped as well, pointing and talking all at once.

Confused, Pamina followed his gaze. Something cold and wet landed on the tip of her nose.

"Oh, it's snowing!" Fiorella's voice echoed above the others.

A chorus of cheers and disgruntled grunts rippled through the crowd. Children laughed and squealed with delight.

Pamina's attention snapped to Lorenzo. "Snow. The mountain pass will be closed then. You'll have to stay! At least until it clears."

He gave her a sad smile. "I'm sure it will be cleared within a few days. If it's just a dusting like this."

Pamina's heart sank. He still wanted to go. Wasn't there anything she could say or do to change his mind?

"I love you, Lorenzo," she blurted, surprising herself.

His eyes widened.

Her face felt as if it was on fire, but she pressed on. "I won't apologize for my boldness. I understand if it makes you uncomfortable, but I had to say it. Even if you leave, I want you to know that. But I hope you don't." Her voice wavered.

"Stay, Lorenzo. Not just for me, but for yourself. You belong in that bakery. You—"

Before she could finish, he kissed her.

His lips pressed against hers, one hand holding her jaw and the other pressed into her back. She kissed him back, growing dizzy with the sensation. Though he hadn't replied with words, she could feel the emotion through his kiss. The love. The need. The pain.

Sorrow gripped her heart. This was a goodbye kiss.

Chapter 20

The Apology

Lorenzo

The snow lasted only a day, and it wasn't deep enough to do much of anything. By the end of the week, it was gone, and Lorenzo's travel plans resumed.

Unable to face Pamina, Lorenzo had steered clear of the bakery, letting Giulia handle the packing and cleaning of their father's back room. It was their last day in Zamerra, and he couldn't put off going into the shop any longer.

With a heavy sigh, he opened the front door and was surprised to find it empty. Where was Pamina?

"Hello?" he called.

"Lor, is that you? I'm back here," Giulia called.

Lorenzo took off his coat to join his sister but paused at the front counter. The displays were filled with delicious treats, and the sugary smell was tantalizing. Pamina's caffé carafe sat on the stovetop, making his throat thicken.

How he would miss drinking the special brew every morning with her. He'd become a successful businessman, buying and selling businesses for profit. But none of that held any appeal to him anymore.

"Lor?" Giulia called again, interrupting his thoughts.

"Coming," he answered, pulling himself away to join her.

The bedroom had been pretty sparse, to begin with, but with most of the furniture gone (sold to the general store), it looked even sadder. Pamina wouldn't be staying there so there'd been no need to keep any of it. Perhaps she could use it for storage or let her sister tear down the wall and connect the two shops.

"Look what I found in one of the drawers, Lor," Giulia said softly, handing him a folded letter.

He took it and gave her a quizzical look. "What is it?"

She motioned toward the paper. "Read it."

Wary of what he would find, he opened it with a frown.

To my dear children, Lorenzo and Giulia,

Lorenzo's gaze snapped to his sister. "What is this? You found it in a drawer? Please tell me you didn't do this."

Giulia scowled at him. "Do what? Write a false letter and try to pass it off as true? Of course, I wouldn't!"

Lorenzo felt a twitch in his jaw. No. His sister wouldn't do something so horrible, which meant the letter was real.

"Read it, Lor," Giulia pressed him.

"I don't want to."

Her eyes narrowed. "Of course, you do. Stop being so insufferably stubborn."

"Why wasn't this with his other papers? His will?"

She shrugged. "I don't know. Maybe because it's not even finished."

A harsh laugh escaped Lorenzo. "Not even finished? He couldn't even bother to finish—"

"Read. It," Giulia ground out.

Despite his better judgment, Lorenzo relented and opened the letter once more.

To my dear children, Lorenzo and Giulia,

I've received a letter from your mother's maid and am appalled that you haven't written me to tell me yourselves. I didn't know your mother was sick and worsening. I've begun preparations to close up my shop and come immediately.

I don't expect my arrival to be met with a warm welcome and I understand why. I'm sorry I wasn't a better father and husband. I tried to be. In the beginning, I thought I could do it, but I'm afraid my melancholy didn't allow me to be the father you needed me to be. Your mother and I both agreed it was better this way. Perhaps, we were wrong. I'm sorry.

I

Lorenzo turned the paper over and found it blank.

"That's all there is," Giulia said softly.

She shook her head. "Isn't it terrible? He must have been planning to come when he had the heart attack. I think he meant to stay this time. He—"

Cold fury swept through Lorenzo. He crumpled up the letter and let it drop to the floor. All the years he'd spent wondering and blaming himself for his father's departure and this was the answer he received?

"Lor?" Giulia asked, eyes full of concern.

"He's sorry. He didn't even finish the letter!"

"Because he died," Giulia snapped back.

Lorenzo shook his head, trying to steady his breathing. "This changes nothing."

"What more do you want, Lor? You can't change the past. You have to stop letting it ruin your future. You're robbing yourself of your own happiness, can't you see that?"

His sister's words rang through his ears, but he didn't want to hear them. He turned to go, but she grabbed his arm.

"Please. I'm begging you, don't make the mistake of leaving like he did. You're going to regret it."

Shaking his sister off, he stormed out of the room, too angry for words. All the memories of growing up and the hardships they'd endured flickered in his mind.

So, what if their father had tried to return? It would have been too late anyway. He wasn't there when Lorenzo needed him. How could he ever forgive that?

Sometimes forgiveness is more for us than it is for the other person. Pamina's voice echoed in his mind.

He threw on his coat and hurried out of the bakery. What if he didn't want to forgive his father? He'd been carrying his anger around for so long, he didn't even know who he would be without it.

That's not true. The voice in his head argued.

With Pamina, he'd seen a glimpse of it. Of a life looking to the future and not the past. A life where he could be happy. Where he could be in love.

That life was in his grasp, but it was slipping fast. He sucked in a lungful of cold air and looked up to the sky. As if he would find the answers there written in the clouds.

But he didn't need such a sign. All he needed was to let go. To let himself heal. *Forgive and forget.*

Just as his mother and Giulia had wanted. Lorenzo still wasn't quite sure how, but he knew someone who would help him. Someone who would love him even through the healing. Someone he loved in return and would fight for every day.

Instead of running away, he'd run forward. Toward the future he wanted and hoped Pamina still did too.

Chapter 21

The Rejection

Pamina

P amina walked alongside their wagon, heart hammering in her ears. The sky was gray and cloudy. She sighed. If only it had continued to snow. She was desperate for more time with Lorenzo.

An ache spread in her chest at the thought of saying goodbye. Could she do it? A tiny part of her was still hopeful that he'd change his mind. Choose to stay with her.

"Are you going to make more pies out of all this pumpkin?" Fiorella's voice interrupted her.

Pamina turned to look at the cart full of crated pumpkin puree. "Pies. Muffins. Bread."

Fiorella grinned from her seat next to Mama. "What about cookies? I can help make those. Does it have to be pumpkin though?"

Pamina smiled. "No. We can make all sorts of things."

With Lorenzo and Giulia leaving and Pamina taking charge, she had promised her little sister she could help in the bakery. As long as she wore her enchanted gloves. Liliana had agreed to double-check everything she made, just in case.

"Would you like to help too, Fina?" Pamina asked, matching the slow wagon.

Her sister had chosen to walk just as she had, but on the other side of the cart. She didn't answer Pamina. Mama looked over to the young girl with a worried frown. They'd never seen Serafina so miserable for so long. Hopefully, Pamina's pie would help.

Nursing her own broken heart, Pamina was determined to see her sister through this hard time. Maybe they could lean on each other to get through it.

Soon, they arrived in town and made their way to the bakery. Pamina's chest swelled as the little shop came into view. She'd come to think of it as a second home, but would it still feel that way tomorrow when Lorenzo was gone?

The ache returned, leaving her unsure and unsteady. She stood for a moment looking into the shop, vaguely aware of her mother and sisters behind her.

"Hello!" Giulia greeted them from the doorway.

Pamina waved back and helped the others unload the wagon. Dante and Liliana came out to join them and offer their assistance.

Inside the bakery looked warm and inviting, but Lorenzo's absence left Pamina cold and disheartened. Wasn't he going to come to say goodbye? The memory of their dance played in her mind, making her heart feel heavy.

"Pamina, why don't you go help Serafina with Fabrizio?" Mama's voice caught her attention.

Serafina frowned. "I don't need help."

Mama shrugged. "Some fresh air will do you both good," she said with a shrewd look.

Pamina didn't want to leave and miss Lorenzo should he come, but she followed Serafina outside anyway. Maybe Mama thought she could help Serafina cheer up.

Fabrizio's hooves clomped loudly as they walked him toward the stables. A gust of wind blew around them, pushing them along.

"I said I didn't need help," Serafina muttered beside her.

Pamina sighed. Aside from making her sister eat enchanted cannoli every day, she wasn't sure what else she could do to help Serafina feel better.

"Would you prefer if I wait here then? Give you some space?" Pamina asked, giving her sister a hesitant smile.

Serafina shrugged. "I don't care what you do."

With that she continued on, not giving Pamina another glance. Pamina watched her go wondering how long this bad mood would persist. Surely, they could find something to help her sister.

"Signorina, you're looking lovely today," a familiar voice called.

Dread unfurled in Pamina's stomach. She turned to see Stefano heading her way.

He frowned. "I said you're looking lovely today."

Pamina forced herself to nod politely in response. A quick look around and she realized they were alone in the alley. Had he been following them?

She started walking once more. If her presence annoyed Serafina, that would be just too bad. She didn't want to be stuck alone with Stefano again.

"Wait," Stefano ordered, grabbing her by the wrist.

Nausea rolled through her. She tried to yank her arm out of his grasp, but he held tightly, squeezing with such force.

"Let go of me. You're hurting my arm!"

Stefano gave her a cold smile. "You were being rude. I much prefer it when you're sweet."

His nearness made her skin crawl. She tried to pull away, but his grip was like iron. Fear spiked through her veins.

Pamina swung her free hand and slapped him hard across the face.

Rage flashed in his eyes. "You. You would reject me?"

"Let go of me!"

"Not until you apologize and make amends. You—" He paused and glanced behind Pamina.

Pamina turned to see Lorenzo stalking toward them. Fury blazed in his eyes.

Suddenly, he was at her side and her shoulders sagged in relief. He grabbed Stefano by the throat and lifted him off the ground. The man sputtered, clawing at Lorenzo's hold.

Pamina gasped. "Lorenzo, don't!"

As much as she despised Stefano, she knew she couldn't let Lorenzo hurt him so. It was unfair, but the law would be on Stefano's side. Goblins were already believed to be too violent, and what Stefano had done to her wasn't bad enough to warrant more than a slap on the wrist.

She touched Lorenzo's arms and tried to pull him off. He glanced at her and blinked as if suddenly remembering she was there.

He dropped Stefano to the ground. The man fell and gasped for breath. Fear lit his face as he looked up to Lorenzo.

"If you ever lay a hand on her or any woman like that again, I will break every bone in your miserable body." Lorenzo's voice was hard.

Stefano's face reddened, but he didn't respond. He shot to his feet and fixed Pamina with an icy glare. "You—"

Before he could finish a bird flew overhead and relieved itself all over his head. Pamina's eyes widened. Lorenzo smiled delightedly.

Stefano yelled in fury and marched off, flinging the white substance to the ground as he went. Pamina spotted a familiar auburn-haired witch at the end of the alley. Serafina smiled at her and continued on. Though she hoped her sister hadn't seen the whole thing, Pamina was glad she seemed to be in a better mood now.

Silence followed and Pamina glanced down at her wrist. Thankfully it wasn't too sore and would heal quickly. Lorenzo's sharp intake made her head snap up.

"He hurt you," he said with rising fury.

Pamina reached for him, her hands on his face. "I'm okay now. Thank you."

His dark eyes stared back at her. "I love you, Pamina."

Now it was her turn to breathe sharply. Warmth filled her. Before she could respond, Lorenzo leaned forward and kissed her softly.

He stepped back and held her gaze. "I'm sorry I couldn't admit it sooner, but I think I fell in love with you from the first day." He snorted. "I never believed in love at first sight, but you changed that. You changed everything."

Tears sprang into Pamina's eyes. "Does this mean you're staying?"

In answer, he closed the distance between them and kissed her once more. Pamina melted into his embrace and returned the kiss.

"Did that answer your question, or do you need more reassurance?" Lorenzo asked, breathless as he withdrew from her.

Pamina smiled so hard her cheeks ached. "I think I need a little more reassurance."

Lorenzo's eyes dipped to her lips, filling her with desire. His arms snaked around her and pulled her tight against his body. Then he kissed her slowly as if savoring her taste.

Heat rushed across Pamina's skin, her heart feeling so light inside her chest.

This, she realized, was what it felt like to be in love.

Chapter 22

A Happy Ending

Lorenzo

B ack in the bakery, Lorenzo was greeted by his sister and Pamina's family. They had all gathered there to say goodbye. He looked around at the somber faces and then back to Pamina, who was smiling from ear to ear.

"What's the matter with everyone?" she asked, noticing all their sorrowful stares.

Lorenzo grunted. "You'd think someone had died."

Giulia marched up to them. "We have something to tell you both. If you will just listen."

Lorenzo's eyebrow arched. He met Pamina's curious look. What were their families up to?

"Now, I know I said I wouldn't meddle, Lor, but if I don't say what I need to and try and convince you one last time to stay, I'll never forgive myself."

His sister's concern warmed him. Though he was tempted to hear out her argument, he'd put her through enough grief.

"Giulia, I'm staying," he said softly.

Her eyes bulged. "You're staying? Really?"

He nodded and glanced at Pamina, who was still holding onto his arm. Giulia clapped and snorted.

"Of course, you tell me this now after I've spent all day drafting the perfect speech," she said with a roll of her eyes.

"You can still give me the full speech. Later. I'm going to go and cancel our tickets."

Giulia shook her head. "Oh, we don't have tickets."

"What?" he asked with a frown.

A chorus of surprise echoed in the bakery. His sister shrugged and met his eyes. "I knew you would come to your senses eventually. I was giving you time."

"So, you had me packing all week for no reason?"

Giulia huffed. "I told you from the beginning you should stay, you oaf."

"But what about your ticket? What about Riccardo?"

Giulia smiled. "He's coming here. As much as I love the city, a nice country wedding sounds much better. Besides, I want him to see the bakery and the pies I helped make."

"Speaking of pie, should we bring some out now?" Pamina asked, eyes on Lorenzo.

Murmurs of approval filled the shop, but Lorenzo was too lost in Pamina's gaze to hear what they said.

He smiled at her. "Pie sounds perfect."

* * *

Lorenzo placed the glass cover over the tray of cannoli and stepped back to admire it. The displays were filled with delicious looking treats. Their sugary aroma and the smell of freshly brewed caffé made him smile.

Though it had taken him a long time to admit he loved working in the bakery, he'd finally accepted it as his calling. He found himself looking forward to going in every day. He couldn't wait to make every single recipe in Pamina's giant cookbook.

He gave her a side glance. It almost seemed too good to be true. All of it had become possible because of Pamina. Being in the presence of the kind witch had rubbed off on him.

She leaned over the counter, putting the final touches of icing on the pumpkin cake. Her eyebrows were knitted together in concentration, her lips pursed. It was a vision Lorenzo wouldn't be able to shake no matter how hard he tried. A memory he would tuck away for when he needed to remember all the good things in life.

Pamina finished and turned to him, eyes widening in surprise. "What is it? Did I mess it up?"

"No. It's perfect," Lorenzo replied, still watching her.

She gave him an amused smile. "You haven't even looked at it yet."

Lorenzo shrugged. "I don't need to. All your masterpieces come out perfect."

Pamina beamed, pushing a mahogany curl out of her face. Lorenzo drank in the sight, wishing he could steal her away from her work. They had been busy all morning and Giulia would be coming in any minute.

Though Giulia hadn't said it, Lorenzo knew she was getting restless in Zamerra. If it hadn't been for the festival and Lorenzo, she probably would have been ready to leave much sooner. Now with Riccardo coming and a wedding to plan, she kept busy, only working here and there in the bakery.

"Do you want to try some?" Pamina asked, holding up a finger she'd dipped in the icing.

Lorenzo's heart stuttered. Heat pooled inside him at her offer. In one movement, he was there in front of her. So close, her sweet smell enveloped him. He took her finger and held it up to his lips, giving her a wicked grin.

Her eyes dropped to his mouth, a look of desire flashing on her face. Slowly, he sucked the icing clean off her finger, body thrumming as she gasped. It was a delicious sound. Even sweeter than the icing that filled his mouth.

Releasing her finger, he pulled her face toward his instead. Before he could kiss her or whisk her away, the door opened and Giulia walked in. Her eyes darted between them. "Are we ready to open the shop today? Everyone is growing anxious."

Lorenzo wagged a finger at her. "That's because you worked them up at the festival."

Giulia snorted. "It wasn't me. It was my pie. Well, the pies I helped with. They can't get enough of them!"

"Yes, well they'll have to wait. Tonight, I was hoping," he glanced at Pamina, "you would join me for dinner?"

"Oh, Lor! That sounds so lovely," Giulia gushed, clapping her hands together.

He shot her a sheepish look. "Well, I actually meant I'd be cooking for just Pamina."

Giulia's eyes gleamed with amusement. "Yes, I know, silly. Don't worry about me. I already made dinner plans with Signor Rossi."

Giving Lorenzo a wink, she turned around and walked right back out of the bakery.

Lorenzo turned to Pamina. "So?"

She smiled at him. "I'd love to have dinner with you."

Lorenzo smiled back, his stomach fluttering. Now he just had to come up with the perfect recipe that would impress a baking witch.

Pamina

"Ooh! Pamina, this pumpkin bread is delicious. I think it's the best you've made yet," Alessia gushed as she took another bite.

Pamina smiled and glanced at Lorenzo. "I didn't make it. That was Lorenzo."

Alessia's eyebrows shot up as she looked at the half-goblin. He shrugged and darted a look to Pamina, lips quirked into a smile.

It wasn't a full smile, but the sight of it made Pamina's heart soar. She hoped for a future filled with many more smiles and delicious food. A lifetime with Lorenzo would make her the happiest woman in the world.

"The bakery was so busy today, I couldn't even see the front counter," Dante announced from his spot beside Liliana.

They'd finished dinner at Pamina's villa and were lounging by the fire, eating dessert. Pamina looked around, feeling happier and fuller than she ever had before. Her gaze met Mama's and the knowing smile on her mother's face made her wonder if she'd known she'd end up beside Lorenzo from the beginning.

Giulia held up a mug of caffé and grinned. "My brother makes a great pumpkin bread, but Pamina's brew is unmatched."

The others murmured their agreement. Pamina's face warmed. It was just as she'd always dreamed for herself. To be surrounded by her family, side by side with someone who saw her and loved her so completely.

Lorenzo's warmth spread through her as she snuggled against him. He looked over at her, his dark eyes piercing through her. Pamina smiled.

She took a bite of the pumpkin bread on her plate and savored it. It was perfectly moist and iced on top. The spices tantalized her taste buds. There was no contentment spell in the recipe this time, but she didn't need it.

Epilogue

Pamina

Pamina stood outside the bakery, rubbing her arms to keep warm. Where was Lorenzo? Or Giulia? The curtain was still closed, and no one had answered her knock. Usually, Lorenzo arrived first.

They'd had a particularly late night though, so perhaps he'd slept in. Pamina smiled at the memory of it. It had been nearly a week, and they'd spent as much time together as possible.

It was unlike him to be late for work.

She glanced around the empty street. Snow coated the roofs of the buildings and the water in the giant fountain in the center of town had frozen. Only the streets had been cleared of the beautiful white blanket. It was a beautiful sight.

As beautiful as it was, Pamina was ready to get inside and start the fire. Turn on the oven and start baking.

The sound of heavy footsteps echoed behind her. She turned to see Lorenzo walking toward her, hands in his pockets and a scowl on his face. He was quite the sight in his long, brown coat and matching hat.

His gaze flickered to her, his scowl turning to a smile. Heat surged through her. When she'd met him, she never would have imagined the grumpy goblin would look at her so.

"You're late," she said with a teasing grin.

Expecting him to tease her back, she was surprised when a worried look flashed across his features. Without a kiss or even a word, Lorenzo headed for the front door and pulled out his keys.

He fumbled with them, nearly dropping them to the ground. Pamina frowned. What had set him in such a sour mood already?

Lorenzo unlocked the bakery and motioned her inside. Pamina walked in, her stomach beginning to churn. Had something happened?

Trusting he'd tell her, she hung up her coat and turned to him expectantly. "Lorenzo? Is everything alright?"

He nodded but said nothing. Pamina watched as he pulled the curtains back and proceeded to start the fire.

She rubbed her hands together, waiting for the shop to warm up. His silence was beginning to worry her. She thought back to yesterday's events to see if she could remember anything that would have upset him.

Fiorella had come to help, and they'd told Lorenzo about her magic. But he hadn't seemed to mind. Was he having second thoughts? Pamina hoped not because Fiorella had been thrilled with the chance to leave the villa and help them in the bakery.

"Lorenzo?" Pamina asked, eyes searching his.

He sucked in a breath and walked toward her, his dark eyes filled with such an intensity, Pamina felt pinned under his stare.

"Pamina, I love you," he started, voice raw.

"Well, I love you too."

He let go of her hand and reached into his pocket. Pamina watched as he pulled out a rolled-up piece of paper.

"What is that? Did you find another letter from your father?"

Lorenzo shook his head and held the scroll out to her. Pamina took it, heart racing. She held it up to the front window to read it in the early morning light.

"Is this... this is the deed to the bakery?"

Lorenzo nodded and motioned for her to continue reading. Her eyes skimmed over the fancy scrawl, snagging on the names in front of her.

She gasped. "You put my name on here."

Her eyes met his. "But what about Giulia?"

"She doesn't want to be an owner, but she did say she expects to eat free here any time she likes."

Pamina laughed. "Of course!"

A smile spread on her face. The bakery had already felt like theirs, but now Lorenzo had made it official. It was a lovely gesture.

She set the paper down on the table and went to kiss him. He held up a hand to stop her.

"You still have to sign at the bottom. There's something else though."

"Oh?"

"There's your name, Pamina."

"Yes, I see it. Thank you. This means so much to me."

Lorenzo took her hands in his. "Yes, but I was hoping, you'd do me the honor of becoming Pamina Bartoli."

Pamina's mouth dropped open. Her heart leapt into her throat. Happy tears sprang into her eyes as she launched herself at him.

"Oh, yes! I would love nothing more," she said, voice wobbling.

Lorenzo drew her to him and laughed. Pamina smiled at the

sound. She loved to hear his deep, rumbling laugh. She didn't think she'd ever get tired of hearing it.

"I would marry you today if we could, but I think one wedding is enough to plan at a time," Lorenzo said as he kissed her forehead.

Pamina looked up at him. "Two, actually. There's Giulia's, and Liliana and Dante are getting married too."

He lifted her chin up to him and stared into her eyes. "You've made me happier than I ever thought I could be. I promise to do my best to make you just as happy, Pamina."

Her smile widened. "You already have."

Lifting herself up on her feet, she pressed her lips against his. He returned her kiss softly at first and then more frantically. His arms wrapped around her, holding her close.

His touch sent a ripple of pleasure and warmth through her and she was lost in the moment. Being loved and loving Lorenzo was all she'd dreamed of and more. Not even her magical caffé or sweets could compare. It wasn't even close.

This was true love. This was true happiness.

The End

Thank you for reading! Serafina's story comes next in *The Wolf's Bride*. You can also read Alessia and Massimo's story in *The Fae's Bride* or Liliana and Dante's story in *The Warlock's Bride*. Each book features a different sister and some of the same characters as well as new ones.

Acknowledgments

First, I'd like to thank my husband for being my partner in all my creative and non-creative endeavors. I wouldn't have such a cute, cozy cover without him

I also want to thank my editor at Cate Edits for working with me. Without her expertise, this book with be riddled with errors.

Finally a big thank you to all my readers who have been following my characters along on their journeys to love and happiness. I truly appreciate all the support and feedback.

Thank you!

Also by R. L. Medina

The Silveri Sisters Series

Book 1: The Fae's Bride

Book 2: The Warlock's Bride

Book 3: The Goblin's Bride

Book 4: The Wolf's Bride

Book 5: The Druid's Bride

YA Fantasy

The Inner World Series

Prequel: Feylin

Book 1: Princess of the Elves

Book 2: Goblin King

Book 3: Fae War

Sign up at my website for a FREE Short story

GRIMM Academy Series

Book 1: Shifters and Secrets

Book 2: Vampires and Werewolves

Book 3: Witches and Wizards

Blood Moon Covenant Series

Book 1: Order

Coming soon...

Book 2: Allegiance

Book 3: Betrayal

About the Author

R. L. Medina is a Bolivian American Fantasy author. At age six, she vowed to hate reading forever. That hate quickly turned to love (or obsession) and by age eight she was filling every note-book with story after story. Now she juggles her time between a busy seven year old and all the characters that demand her time. When she's not exploring all the Sci-fi/Fantasy worlds in her head, she enjoys life with her family in Florida.

Check out her website at www.rlmedina.com for a free story, giveaways, and updates!

You can also find her embarrassing herself on TikTok @bookdragonlife and the social media channels below:

Printed in Great Britain
by Amazon

58954126R00116